a sacred devotion

As the clock strikes midnight, Shannon is surrounded by celebration and warmth. But in her heart, there's cold fear. Her relationship with Mitch is at a crossroads, and it's time to act on her New Year's resolution to tell him everything.

The tragedy that drove her to escape to Petrie's Crossing. How she came to own Trinkets. And her quest to use her gift and return each item in her secret box to its rightful owner.

One of which, she now knows, belongs to Mitch. Which means it's time to reveal to him every dark secret she's been holding back. And hope he'll understand why.

As their relationship wobbles on shaky ground, Shannon's world tilts once again with the appearance of a face from her painful past, bearing a message she's not ready to hear. Leaving her wondering if the roots she's put down will hold her firm in Petrie's Crossing, or tear loose and send her running once again.

a sacred devotion

Lost Trinkets Series Book Six

Sherrie Lea Morgan

Village Publishing

ACWORTH, GEORGIA

Sherrie Lea Morgan/Village Publishing
PO Box 2519
Acworth, Georgia/USA 30102
www.sherrieleamorgan.com

This is a work of fiction. Names, places, characters and incidents are either the product of the author's imagination or are used fictitiously, and any resemblance to any actual persons, living or dead, organizations, events or locales is entirely coincidental.

Book Layout © 2017 BookDesignTemplates.com

a sacred devotion/The Lost Trinkets Series Book Six/Sherrie Lea Morgan. – 1st ed.
Editor: Lindsey Loucks
Cover for this book done by Yocla Designs
ISBN 978-1-949256-11-6

I'm dedicating this book to Tessa. Thank you for our early morning pre-coffee chats and support. It means more to me than I can ever say. We're half-way there, girlfriend!

psychometry (sī käm ə trē) noun

     1. the ability to discover facts about an event or person by touching inanimate objects associated with them.

manifestation (man ə fes tāSH(ə)n) noun

     d: an occult phenomenon; specifically: *materialization*

Medium (mēdē ə m)

     1. A person claiming to be in contact with the spirits of the dead and to communicate between the dead and the living

psy·chic (/ s̸īkik/) noun

     1. A person considered or claiming to have psychic powers; a medium.

ghost (gōst) noun

     1. The soul of a dead person believed to be an inhabitant of the unseen world or to appear to the living in bodily likeness.

Forensic Psychic

     1. A person who investigates crimes by using purported paranormal psychic abilities.

contents

Chapter One

"Five...four...three...two...one. Happy New Year!" Everyone who stood shoulder to shoulder in the large living room of Mitch's home cheered, then turned and hugged each other. His no kissing policy for this party rocked. Memories of being single at parties in the past flickered through my mind. Nothing like watching a pack of people kissing each other only to be forced to acknowledge you were closing out another year without someone to kiss to really drive home the idea of starting a new year alone. I didn't mind being alone. The sad desperate looks of other singles punched me in the gut every time though. Well, most of the people at Mitch's house knew before the party started of the rule and reveled in it. From Andy's teen boys to Aurora's eighty-year old father grinned and gathered hugs. My lips lifted as the sweet warmth of the emotions in the room washed over me. Bobby wrapped his beefy large arms around me and nearly suffocated me in a bear hug. Mitch followed suit.

"Happy New Year, sweetheart," he whispered in my ear. "Kisses to follow later after we boot the crowd."

I giggled and nodded. I couldn't wait.

As the roar dimmed to a light chatter of voices, Mitch weaved a path toward the front door and lifted his hand ringing a large bell. Everyone quieted and turned as one to face him. "Now, remember folks, we have over fifty empty to-go boxes in the dining room." Placing an arm across the shoulders of the recently arrived priest standing beside him, he continued, "Father O'Brannon has his van warmed up outside ready to deliver food to the homeless on the streets in Augusta tonight. No one leaves without filling a minimum of two boxes and delivering them to the van." He grinned showing those white perfect teeth of his. "As well as passing my sobriety test. I've got bus boys being paid overtime to drive you folks' home if you need it, so take advantage of it, for their sakes."

Everyone cheered, then nearly a third moved to line up in the dining room, grabbing and filling their required two boxes. Most everyone filled at least three, some four. I had to hand it to him... it was a fantastic idea.

"Nice party," Steph whispered in my head.

"Yeah."

"He's a keeper you know."

"Yep."

"New Year, new resolutions. You got yours, right?"

I sighed. "Yeah. First thing tomorrow morning, I'll begin the process."

"Good. I'm gonna go head out and celebrate with the other ghosts. Apparently, they all gather near the graveyard to say goodbye to departing spirits. Why they don't do this on all Hallows Eve when the veil is the thinnest is beyond me." A soft chuckle followed her announcement, then nothing. She'd dissipated like vapor in the breeze.

I headed toward the kitchen to help Nancy start the cleaning process.

"How's it going?" I asked, filling the sink with soap.

"Great, you?"

I slid a glance her way and noted the rosy pink tint to her cheeks. "Good. But something tells me you've got a specific reason for being 'great'. So, what's up?"

Nancy blinked. "I'm glad we're friends now."

"But?"

"But this is still new, and I'd like to keep it to myself for a bit?"

"Sure thing. I'm happy for you though," I gave her a quick half hug.

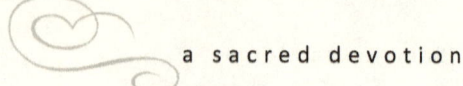

Sounds of departing guests floated in around us as we washed and rinsed dishes.

"Why are we washing these? Mitch's dishwasher is top notch," Nancy asked.

"Because, this way, he won't have to empty it and some of these dishes belong to Marnie and the Haygoods. They'll want them before they leave."

"Got it."

Marnie chose that moment to join us. "Any chance mine got in the first round?"

"Yep," I responded and handed her the dishes she'd brought to the party.

"Perfect. I'm calling it a night. Chloe is coming down for a few more days before she heads back to that fancy art school."

I spun around. "Is she truly liking it? It's gotta be hard for you to have your only daughter living so far away."

"Since she arrived home for the holidays, it's been bearable. I'm thinking of going up for a visit next month, as a surprise."

"I think that'd be nice."

"I'd call first," Nancy warned.

Marnie frowned. "Why?"

Nancy grinned before responding. "Um...twenty-something living out of town and away from Mom for the first time?"

Marnie's eyes widened. "Ah, give her time to clean up a bit?"

Nancy shook her head. "That among other things. At least give her a week's notice or so."

Marnie nodded. "Okay, I will. Good night you two," she said before turning and heading out of the kitchen.

After everyone left, Mitch tugged my hand and we headed toward the master bedroom on the main floor. I loved this house with its wrap around porch and French doors in nearly every room leading out to said porch.

"Oh, I have a surprise for you," he said and steered away from the bedroom down the hall and my body trembled. *Drat*. The room meant sweet things and putting if off made me antsy. I followed him anyway. What surprise did he have in store? "Close your eyes," he said stopping in front of the reading room I'd seen before. How could this be a surprise? I did as he instructed and waited. The sound of the knob turning along with the door swinging open frayed the edges of my patience. "Okay, open your eyes."

I did, then gasped. He'd rearranged the room and cleared out some of the furniture. A large wooden desk sat facing the side windows and a plush purple paisley armchair sat against the opposite wall. Small wooden filing cabinets, no bookshelves, sat against the back wall. A long flowing sheer cloth with fairy lights softly lit the corner near the lounge. So, inviting. I stepped inside and scanned the room. "I like what you've done in here." My eyes widened at the stone incense holder sitting in the corner of the desk. I tilted my head and glanced back at him.

"You've made this a very peaceful room. Is this your new office?" Why would this be a surprise for me?

"Not for me, silly. For you," he whispered.

My stomach dropped and my heart hit hard against my ribs. He'd asked me a couple months ago to move in and I asked to wait. Was I being given a time limit or deadline here?

"You don't like it."

"No, I love it," I said plastering a smile across my face. "But—"

"—I know, " he interrupted. "You said you needed time. I understand. I've been meaning to get this room updated anyway and thought you'd like to see what would be waiting for you once you made your decision."

"Like saying no would mean you did all this for nothing?" I waved my arm. I stiffened. "Ultimatums never worked well for me."

"It's not an ultimatum."

"Isn't it?"

He frowned and crossed his arms in front of his chest. "No. I guess I misunderstood. I thought you asked for time to get used to the idea with the answer being an eventual yes. Apparently, I'm wrong," he said then spun around and left.

I blew out a breath. Good move. But, dang it. I didn't do ultimatums and that is exactly what this is, whether he wanted to admit it or not. I stomped after him. How dare he? I headed into the bedroom and he wasn't there. Where'd he go? "Mitch?" I called out.

"In the kitchen," he said.

When I arrived, he'd opened a beer and was in the process of wiping down the kitchen counters. "We did that already," I said.

He continued onto another counter. "Some areas were missed."

I stood there. He shifted from one counter to the next with jerky movements. He'd run out of counter soon enough. I'm the one upset, so why did he behave as though he had the right...no, never mind. This is bologna. He dropped the rag into the sink, lifted his bottle and took a long drought of the amber liquid without looking at me. Fine.

"I'm sorry I ruined your surprise."

"No worries. It was my fault for assuming you'd like it."

"I told you I liked it," I said lifting then dropping my hands.

"You did. Listen, I know both our places are closed tomorrow, but I think this party wiped me out. I'm heading to bed," he set his half empty bottle on the counter and shifted to scoot past me. He paused, gave me a quick peck on the cheek then moved on.

I jerked back. Did that mean I'm dismissed? Did I need to go home? I grabbed his bottle off the counter and sidled up to the sink. My plans of making love all night and sleeping in went down the drain along with the rest of his beer as I poured it out. *Perfect*. My shoulders dropped and I rubbed my face over my hands. Ugh. I let my gaze drift around the place. Could I live here and keep my secret? No. Living here meant I'd wake up next to him every morning, to his brown gold-flecked eyes and curly hair. I'd have good food every day, but at what cost? I couldn't even consider moving in until he knew everything. Every dark secret I had. If they wouldn't create a public outcry, I might be able to do it. It wouldn't be fair to him or to us. I loved him.

Steph? I asked in my mind. No answer. Guess her ghost friends made better company for her right now anyway. I didn't blame her. I sucked in a deep breath, grabbed my purse from the entryway and paused. I'd left my overnight bag in the bedroom. I'd get the darn thing later. Staring at the ground, I headed home to sleep in my own bed...alone.

Chapter Two

Sharp stabs dug in my armpit as Harmony did her morning cat routine of patty caking. Ouch. The burn pulsated along with the pounding in my head. The throbbing headache wrapped around from my temples to my neck. Happy New Year, my butt. Harmony purred and shifted away, jumping onto the floor and swaggering out of the room, her tail swishing along with her gait. I clenched my eyelids against the winter morning glare and crawled out from beneath my covers. Making my way blindly to my bathroom, I felt along the counters until my fingers touched the bottle containing pills to push the pain away. Swallowing two, I stripped and jumped in the shower. The heat of the water and steam worked its magic in my sinus cavity, clearing them along with relaxing the tense muscles of my neck. I sighed loudly simply because I could. Within an hour, I'd dressed and shuffled down the hall to my office above Trinkets. The cushions of my desk chair let out a whoosh when I plopped down. Leaning my head back, I waited and breathed slow even breaths until the medicine drove the headache farther away

from my mind. I sat and tugged the little chain to turn on my small lamp. Keeping my mind blank, I lit the nag champa incense, then the various candles I had placed around the room. Tugging out the crystals, I placed them along the exterior edge of my desk until I'd depleted the stack. Palms flat on the wooden surface, I closed my lids and forced my mind to blank, my shoulders to drop and my muscles to relax.

Within minutes, the soundtrack of my special mediation music still echoed throughout the room, calming my random thoughts. I stood and stretched before returning to my seat and tugging out Aunt Caroline's little box of trinkets. Was it fate? Or more like a curse? No, the path set before me of whose directions I chose to follow. One by one, I'd been returning items from this little box she'd hidden from everyone but myself. I studied the remaining items she'd won from her special poker games with her lover years ago. Items people pawned at his shop which he then refused to resell. I suppose he hoped one day the owners would return or come to claim such personal items. After all, some were obvious heirlooms. They never did. So, here I am tracking the rightful owners down and returning their heirlooms using my gift of psychometry. Gift. Yes, it's a gift, though I can't lie, some days it behaved more like a curse. My resolution may end up causing me heartache, but I'm done hiding from Mitch. This resolution will be kept, even if it jeopardizes losing the one man who made me feel special and loved.

Sliding on my gloves, I nudged aside the old broken watch, hair combs, and pearl earrings to grasp the signet ring. I held it under the light and studied the gold band and scripted letter "C" with its swirls on the top. The letter and prior vision I'd had confirmed it belonged to a Calabretti once. Since Mitch was the only Calabretti left in town, it needed to be given to him. I set it on the cloth I'd placed in the center of my desk, returned the box to my drawer and tugged out my small notebook along with Aunt Caroline's diary. Flipping to the page I'd written the description of my first vision of the ring, I scanned the words. *Always Calabretti.*

I tugged off my gloves. Time for another reading. Maybe this vision would provide more answers. One way or the other, it'd be nice to have as much information in my arsenal as I could before facing Mitch. I blew out a long breath and held the ring. An image of an older man weeping beside a hospital bed drifted into my mind, then quickly faded out before my mind blanked. Okay, so an old man with sick old lady. Mitch's grandparents? *Ugh.* I slipped on my gloves and replaced the ring in the box.

Rising, I searched for Hank's book which Maggie had finished and returned. Although he'd sent me the digital copy of his book before he published it, I hadn't read it all from beginning to end. I'd only completed searches of the portions related to my involvement in the search for little Timmy Barns and the ultimate discovery of his corpse. My gut groaned. I needed food first, before moving forward with the next thing on my to do list. I located the blasted thing under the sales counter downstairs in the shop. Holding it carefully between glove covered hands, I returned upstairs and set it on my desk. Removing my gloves, I headed into the kitchen to make some toast. Harmony joined me and twined her body in figure eights around my ankles as I waited for the toaster to finish its job. Once it did, I slathered peanut butter over the tops and grabbed a glass of milk to stand at the counter and eat. I rolled my head to each shoulder keeping the tension beat back. Cleaning up, I paused, stroking Harmony's calico fur, taking pleasure in the feel of her soft coat, then marching back to my office.

Time to face the fears. Pretend it's someone else's life blowing up. I grabbed the book, stretched out on my couch and opened to page one. I rubbed the crystals I'd grabbed along with the book in my left hand as I turned the pages with my right. He'd began his story from the day before Timmy went missing. Trying to keep my jaw from clenching, I kept turning the pages and reading. *Stay calm. Breathe through it. Keep reading.* When Hank wrote on explaining how desperate the boy's parents were, they approached to the local psychic shop searching for someone, anyone who might have the gift to help them, I sucked in my breath. Here it goes. Unbidden images of that fateful day in New Day Metaphysical came flooding into my mind.

Mr. & Mrs. Barns walking hesitantly into the store as most of the customers did, failed to catch my attention as much as the dark circles under their reddened eyes. Sadness enveloped this couple and reached out to my senses. A need to ease that sadness stole over me. Martha Romana tapped my arm lightly.

"Breathe through it and let it fall away from you. Let me see how we might be able to help them, yes?"

I dipped my head in agreement. Martha was our most gifted medium in residence. Although some days I believed I was obtaining the level of her skill, if not exceeding it. My regular customers paid well and were always so grateful for my readings. I loved helping them find lost things. The two times I'd helped some probation officers increased my popularity. Martha and I had recently returned from

a psychic forensic class taught in Chicago. We both did well and the cold case I'd been assigned and solved was quickly followed by several contacts from the instructors' private group of substantiated mediums. Life was good. She approached the couple and after whispering for a few minutes, led them to her room in the back where she did her private readings.

I checked the schedule and discovered I'd have the afternoon free. Before I could gather my gear, Martha called me back to join her. Why?

Chapter Three

Blinking and shoving the images from my mind, I inhaled deep letting the air filling my lungs to calm my hammering heart. My personal nightmare, no, mine and Timmy's parents' nightmare started then. The memories rushed in, tumbling and running rampant in my mind. Meeting the two distraught parents of the missing eight-year-old boy. Their only child taken by a stranger. Scenes of my receiving vision after vision from holding his little toy elephant. A young child's fear flowing within my body and yet I experienced a sense of hope. Hope due to his breathing and crying confirming his life was still intact with each vision. Memories of a specific place in my vision where he waited, crying for his mommy and daddy. Our convincing the police to let me show them and the gathering of special units rushing into the woods spending minutes which seemed like hours searching for the one tree standing prominently in my visions. A long breath slipped past my dry lips when I continued reading about the hope and despair his parents experienced while working with a young and inexperienced psychic whose

Hank's writing tugged me into the terror of the days leading up to the very moment little Timmy's body was finally found. I fought to escape his words, his world, my past without success. Tears filled my eyes and I blinked them away as the book neared the end and described the catastrophic cacophony of cries emanating from Timmy's parents following my final vision which included absolute terror, shock and the sudden loss of life. I breathed Timmy's last breath with him while he died at the hands of a monster. No one gave me the opportunity to breathe and recover from my last vision there in the small clearing as they descended upon me with their accusations, distaste, and disgust. It was as though they figured I intentionally gave hope where there was none to give. My mind reeled when I recalled the race to escape the jeering crowd casting their callousness my way until I escaped and fell apart.

Hank hadn't included that part in his book. No, he'd left out the following days of harassment by everyone who spotted me, the reports of those calling me names, spitting at me and the type of threats I'd received soon after. He didn't include the ostracism I faced from my fellow psychics and

Hank had

subsequent removal from the one place I believed to be home.

I closed Hank's book, set it on the floor, leaned back and let the darkness drop its dismal shroud across my shoulders while releasing another torrent of tears from an endless pit which never failed to arrive when the images of my last contact with Timmy appeared.

"Shan, I'm here," Steph's voice whispered in my ear. "I can't get inside your mind. Can you hear me?"

A chill covered my body as her ghostly presence surrounded me. I dipped my head in the only way I could communicate.

"I'm here now."

"I know," I returned before jumping up and began shaking my arms, gulping in air, before quickly releasing it pushing the darkness away. I opened my lids, walked toward the window and lifted my face to the sky. "I'm okay."

"Sure?" She asked worriedly.

"Yeah," I pointed toward the couch where the book sat. "I read it."

Silence.

I peered down watching the smattering of people sitting and chatting at Mitch's diner across the street below. I did it. I read the book. I spun around and

faced the white misty form of my twin. "I read his book."

"And?"

"And I lived," I said, then returned to sit. "It wasn't easy, but I will admit Hank did a good job."

"Now what?" She asked.

"Now, I move past it."

I placed the book into my bag and headed toward the bathroom to wash my face. Steph's ghostly form floated after me.

"What are you going to do with the book?"

"I'm going to give it to Mitch to read."

"Good."

"I hope so," I said drying off and changing my shirt, before returning to the office. I grabbed my bag, "I really hope so. This can go south in so many ways."

"It can. You ready for that?"

I faced her, tipping my head and replied. "It's a new year. A few months and we will mark our first anniversary of moving to Petrie's Crossing. It's time, don't you think?"

"You got this. If it goes south," she shrugged her shoulders, "You still have me."

I grinned. "Yes, and that is probably the one thing that has kept me out of the looney bin all these years."

She chuckled. "I'd still be with you. Even there."

"I know," I said, then headed downstairs calling out a goodbye to Harmony as I left through the back door. I walked up the back alley toward Storm Street, turned right and made my way across Main and into Calabretti's Diner. Threading my way through patrons and staff, I searched for Mitch among the cooks in the back kitchen. Mitch stood stirring a large pot of marinara sauce while chatting with his sous chef who presently sautéed garlic and onions. He turned his head the moment I entered scanning the length of my body before returning his gaze to mine. He continued talking, although now watching me make my way toward him. He didn't frown nor switch his gaze away from me. *Please let that be a good sign. Please let this work.*

The aromas twirled about me making my head dance with scents of tantalizing Italian dishes. Straightening my shoulders, I approached the man who made my insides melt with a simple word and laid a hand against his back. He muttered something to the other worker and turned toward me lifting his chin and tipping his head indicating the back area. I followed, swallowing past the lump in my throat. This had to be done. Better now than later and get it over with. He tugged me into a small corner and raised a brow. With shaking hands, I lifted Hank's book out of my bag and handed it to him.

He scanned the cover and kept silent. Great.

"This is for you so you can understand where I'm coming from. I think it's important."

He nodded and slid a quick check on the kitchen. "I'm sorry, we've got a party of thirty coming in later and I need to get back in there."

"I thought you intended to close today, or at least take the day off."

"Not closing. We got a call begging us to open. Besides, nothing else to do but work today."

I bit my lip as the sharp stab struck my chest. Yep, he's mad.

"I'm sorry," I offered. What else could I say?

"Things happen. I need to go," he said shifting his feet ready to turn away.

"Will you call me later?" *Drat*. Was that pathetic? Yes. But nothing stopped the words from tumbling out of my mouth.

"Sure," he said, then walked away after setting the book on the top shelf along with unused pans.

Perfect. I'd handed him my nightmare and it now sat discarded among the unwanted pots. Did that mean I'd be unwanted soon, too? Pressing my lips together, I slipped out the back door unprepared to face the curious townsfolk peeking and whispering over their manicotti while I walked past them. After crossing the street, I returned home the same way I left. Slumping in my office chair with my face in my hands, I let the ache inside me release, crying…again, like a teenager whose boyfriend decided to shun her for some perceived wrong. Rejection hurt no matter how old one got.

I sat there as the afternoon sun moved over the sky. I sat there until the light turned dim through my windows, then I rose. *Move on, girlfriend.* I had a trinket which needed returning and it will get returned. If I lose a man in the process, I will not die. But, drat if I'm going to sit here like a bump on a log. Heading to the kitchen, I fixed dinner for myself, then Harmony. I stroked her soft fur when she finished and planned my evening. Long hot meditation bath followed by reading Aunt Caroline's diary for any evidence I could find on Mitch's ancestors that I saw in my vision. His grandfather mainly, as he had to be the man I saw. Rarely did I receive images of anyone older than two generations back.

As I meandered around my office an hour later, the music from the drum circle track filled the air with soft harmonic beats. Three lit incense sticks, one candle and a snuggle session with Harmony later, I finally tugged out Aunt Caroline's diary and began searching the pages for any mention of the Calabretti's. Grinning, I leaned forward holding the book under the lamp. Here we go.

Today, I visited Alessandria Calabretti. Her health is deteriorating faster than anyone expected. Each day that passes, her skin becomes paler, her words more jumbled, and the veins in her arms more pronounced. So heartbreaking to see a once vibrant woman succumb to such a devastating illness. When it is my time to go, I pray I go quickly in the night while asleep. I do not wish anyone to experience what poor Jack Calabretti is experiencing. His face is consistently marked with deep worry lines. How awful to see one's spouse in such a state? I wish there was something I could do, but I cannot. It is all I can do to remain hopeful in my own life.

Chapter Four

Later that evening, I lay in bed reflecting on the words written by Aunt Caroline. Mitch's grandmother appeared to have suffered an illness making her weak during her last days. How awful it must have been. Had Mitch and she been close like my relationship with my own grandmother? Staring at the ceiling, I snuggled farther under my quilt and shifted slightly when Harmony hopped up and began her nightly ritual of patty-caking my side. I breathed in tandem to her purrs for a bit before checking the time. Would he call me tonight as he said? A long sigh escaped once Harmony finished and crawled up to curl herself around the top of my head and began cleaning my hair. Her tongue tugged the strands away from my forehead.

The phone rang and I jumped before reaching over to answer.

"I'm trying to understand why you would keep the fact of your history from me. Is it because you're afraid I'd hate the publicity your secret occupation would cause?"

My heart beat hard inside my chest making me gulp before responding. No hello or anything. Okay, direct and straight to the point, then. "Yes," I said crossing my fingers. *Please let him understand.*

"You're right, especially if you're well known. I know the book being a bestseller might draw a lot of attention. But there aren't too many folks around here who would gush about it."

I frowned. He didn't sound too angry. "Are you angry?" I needed to know.

"I won't lie to you. I am disappointed more about you keeping this from me. It's not likely to bring a bunch of reporters or strangers to town searching for an interview, right?" He paused. "So, why did you keep it a secret?"

"Because it might one day bring them?" Especially if they found out where I'd run to hide.

"How many books do you have out there? I'm more curious about that and why you'd choose a man's name as a pseudonym. Is that a common practice?"

I squeezed my lids shut. He thought I was the author.

"You didn't read the book?"

"No, I'm not a big book reader. Don't you have fans that read your books and tell you if they like it? Is it really that important that I like your writing too?

I mean, I'll support you, but the subject of this book isn't something I'm honestly interested in reading about."

My fingers chilled as a sour taste formed in my mouth. I could let him believe...no. Making a resolution and dropping it is the chicken's way out. "Mitch, I'm not an author. I didn't write that book." There I said it. Now my world will fall apart.

"Oh. Then why did you give me this book?"

"I need you to read it. Please. It's important you read it all the way through."

"Why don't you simply tell me? I don't like games."

That's it. I combed my icy cold fingers through my hair, barely resisting the urge to tug at the strands sliding through my fingers. Through clenched teeth, I responded, "Because for you to truly understand who I am and what I've been through, you must read this story. It is better explained through that book than any way I could possibly tell you right now."

"Fine," he snapped. "No need to yell."

"I didn't mean to yell." *Yes, I did.* Didn't he understand how hard this hit me? No, he wouldn't. How could he know I'm laying my life and my secret open to him? I'm risking everything and he wasn't getting it. I released a pent-up breath. Mr. Calm and Logical didn't get the point. "Please, read the book.

Then, we can talk, and you can decide if you still want to be with me."

Silence fell between us allowing static alone buzzing in my ear along with the blood rushing through my head pulsating at my temples.

"This book is that important?" He asked.

"Yes."

"Then I will. Goodnight," he said then disconnected.

The pain like a thousand drums beating against my skull made me press my fingers to my temples to alleviate the tension. It didn't help. My gut burned with nausea. I jumped out of bed amidst Harmony's protest symphony of meows and rushed into the bathroom to empty my stomach. Perspiration broke out along my forehead when I bent over the bowl. Dang it. Making my way in the dark, I turned on the shower, setting the water at its hottest point on the dial, then stripped, stepped in, dropped to the floor and sat there in a fetal position while the droplets blended with the tears pouring down my cheeks. When did I turn into such a crybaby? My shoulders shook as I curled there under the spray and sobbed for the loss of a little boy, his parents' grief and my own loss. *Stephanie. I should have died instead of you.*

When the water turned cold, I remained letting the numbness crawl from my toes to my head. Slowly, I rose on shaky legs to turn off the now ice-cold deluge and stepped out, I dried myself off and crawled back to bed seeking the warmth of my quilt. Harmony joined me, lying across my chest and placed her head on my shoulder, purring loudly. I forced my mind to blank and welcomed the darkness of nothingness in my head.

****

Thursday morning's winter brightness lit my room along with Harmony's meows demanding food. I tugged my pillow over my head and remained still. *Not now. I'm not ready yet.* Her piercing claws poked through the quilt at the sensitive part of my feet between my toes. *Ouch.* I plucked my legs up to avoid her next attack and got jabs in my ankles. *Great.* I threw off the pillow, sat and glared at those blue eyes of hers.

"I'm awake now, thank you very much." Swinging my legs off the sides, I paused as she hopped down and swaggered out the door meowing her way toward the kitchen. Make her wait or go feed her now? Sounds of items being knocked off the counter hitting the floor carried into room. Demanding little tabby cat. I shuffled my way to feed her, stretching

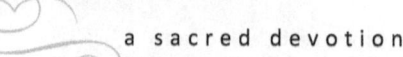

my arms above me when a loud yawn released itself from my lungs. Another bowl toppled to the floor as I entered. "I'm here already. Stop knocking everything down," I said filling her bowl, then headed back toward my bedroom. I let last night's conversation with Mitch meander its way back into my mind. What a disaster.

"I thought you were going to move on and forward," Steph said while floating near the window as I made up the bed.

"Why do you think I'm not?" I asked, the heat crawled its way up my neck and into my cheeks. I averted my face while I picked up discarded clothing, tossed them in the hamper and quickly threw on clean clothes.

"I popped in to see if you were okay last night and saw you in the shower."

"A moment of weakness," I mumbled.

"Aren't you tired of them?"

I straightened and stared at her for a bit first, before nodding. "I am. But it's not like it's something I can always control."

"Try harder," she whispered.

I raised my eyebrows. "Oh sure, that's easy for you to say."

She grinned. "Love you. You got this," she said before evaporating.

Chapter Five

The bell from downstairs rang and I jumped. Maggie had arrived to open the shop. I hiked downstairs and started the water to make tea, before joining her at the counter. I waited while she prepped the computer and got set up for the day. She glanced my way while she shuffled papers, until she paused raising a brow.

"Good morning," She said.

"Morning. How's your grandmother doing?" I asked. Why the raised brow? Did I forget to brush my hair? I patted my head. *Dang cat.* Tugging out a band, I swept the unruly mess into a ponytail.

Maggie grinned. "She's excited, she received notice that she's moved up the list and is now in the top five for receiving a place of her own at the assisted living place I told you about."

"That's great."

She turned toward me. "So, what's your New Year's resolution? I'm guessing it has nothing to do with getting your hair cut?"

I winced. "Harmony woke me and, in my rush to come chat, I...never mind. It wasn't that bad."

She shrugged. "No, just teasing you. So, your resolution?"

"You tell me yours first," I insisted.

"I've decided that I'm going to stay positive about my grandmother's relocation and that when it's time, I'll find a place of my own."

"You're not planning on staying at the house you're at now?"

"No. I've been helping my grandmother make her rent, but the landlords are wanting to sell it as soon as she moves out."

"Oh, I'm sorry. You have any places in mind?"

"Nope," she raised a hand, "and I'm not thinking about it right now. This is me, trying to stay positive here."

I nodded. "Got it."

Silence.

"Well?" She asked and when I blinked at her, she smiled. "Yours?"

"Oh," I said and shrugged. "I've decided to tell Mitch everything."

She gaped. "Everything...like your gift and your history before moving here? That everything?"

"Yep. I gave him the book the other night and asked him to read it." I let out a small breath, before continuing. "At first, he thought I meant that I was the author and that I was hiding it from him."

She frowned. "Uh-oh."

"Yeah, uh-oh is right. I told him that I wasn't the author, but that I needed him to read the book."

"Think he'll figure it out? He's smart, but without any hints...he might not."

"If not, I'll have to explain. But at least he'll have most of the background information and I'll only need to connect the dots for him."

She tilted her head to the side. "Speaking of your gift. You doing another item from your little box?"

"I am actually."

She clapped her hands "Oh good. Can I help? I mean, what is it first?"

"It's a signet ring that belongs to Mitch's family."

She gasped.

"I know," I responded quickly. "I figure if I'm going to tell him everything, he might require proof and since I have something that I'll be giving to him, I might as well do that one now."

"So how do you know it belongs to his family?"

I gave her a wry grin. "It has the letter 'C' engraved on it."

"C for Calabretti. What if it's not for Calabretti, but for someone else? I mean, how can you be sure?"

"Because I also did a vision for it and the older man in my vision looked like an older version of

Mitch. I'm thinking it must have been his grandfather's ring."

"Why not his dad?"

"The guy seemed too old to be his dad. Plus, my aunt mentioned in her diary about his grandmother being sick, so it fits the vision." The tea pot whistled from the kitchen. "Let me get a cup of tea and we'll talk more." I fixed my cup and called out, "Did you want one too?"

"No, thanks" Maggie responded.

I returned and stood next to the counter sipping my tea. "So, what do you know about Mitch's family?"

"Hasn't he told you all about himself yet?"

"Some. I mean," I set my cup on the counter. "I know he took over the diner about three years ago when his dad retired. I think because his parents wanted to be able to travel and visit his siblings. Cameron and his wife came down to stay for a while to learn the ropes of the day to day operations of running a diner because they want to open one where they live in North Carolina." I took a sip, then continued. "He hasn't told me much more about the rest of his family."

Maggie dipped her chin, then glanced my way. "I know he was engaged when he gained ownership of the diner. I think that was the reason his engagement failed, but I don't know for certain."

I leaned forward. "He hasn't told me much about his ex-fiancée. What was she like?"

"I didn't know her very well as she was older than me and ran with a totally different crowd than I did."

"Crowd?"

"She grew up in Augusta and her family was considered middle class. I'd heard she hated that and aspired to move up in society. She traveled to Petrie's only to participate in founders' events. I think she hoped to snag herself a founder with deep pockets," she paused, then continued. "To be fair, she was very nice and very attractive. I only met her twice and both times, she talked about travelling and escaping the small-town life."

"And she accepted a proposal from Mitch? He's so ingrained with the people here and it's obvious to everyone how committed he is to Petrie's. Heck, everyone in town knows him. Did she really think he'd take her away from here? "

"I think she did. That is…until he inherited the diner."

"Oh, so you think she broke it off because of that?"

"I'm sure that was a big point in the negative column for her. Other than that, I don't honestly

know much else about his family history." She winked then continued, "Also, most of what I told her was gossip other than I what I heard myself. Not sure how accurate that could be."

"I get it."

"Can I see the ring?" Maggie asked.

"Sure," I swung away and headed upstairs. Once I slid on my gloves, I retrieved the gold ring and returned to the kitchen. "Come in here to see it. I don't want to take a chance a customer might spot it."

She joined me in the kitchen and held out her hand. I placed it in her palm, and she studied the engraved front then peered closer to the interior portion of the ring.

"There's an inscription," she whispered.

"Always Calabretti," I said. "I saw it earlier."

"When will you show it to Mitch?" She asked handing it back.

I turned the ring around in my hand, then glanced at her. "I'm not sure yet. I'd like to have more information before I get to that point. So far, I've only had one vision and it's of the older man. I did find out through some research that Mitch's grandmother was very ill."

Maggie nodded. "She died when Mitch was younger, I think. I don't know of what or how, though."

"Well, I'll try more visions in between dealing with my stupid resolutions for the New Year."

The front door of Trinkets opened, and I glanced over to the customer who entered. At first, I blinked. No, it can't be. I gaped as the woman entered slowly and gazed around the store. Maggie rushed toward the counter and called out a welcome. The woman turned and my breath caught in my throat while my mind blanked. A sudden coldness swept over my body and my pulse raced. I turned to run before stopping myself. I can't run. My hand automatically rose to my throat and pressed against my chest to ease the pounding of my heart. I froze and tried to take a breath, but it caught in my lungs. The woman smiled at Maggie before she shifted her gaze in my direction and locked on me.

"Well, I almost didn't recognize you," she said in the once calming lilting voice she carried and moved toward me. As she passed Maggie, she lifted one side of her lips and winked. "I'm a friend of Shannon's from Birmingham."

Maggie's gasp followed the woman as she approached me. I couldn't budge if I tried. I forced air

into my lungs and wrapping my arms across my front, I nodded.

"Martha," I said in a wavering voice. "What are you doing here?"

Martha Romana, medium, psychic teacher and my mentor dipped her head before responding. "I received a message to check on you." She shrugged, lifted then dropped her hands. "So, here I am."

"Here you are," I whispered. "Who gave you the message?" Not that I truly wanted to know. No, I didn't. Not at all. I shook my head. "Never mind. Don't tell me. I'm surprised to see you."

"I can tell by your white face and frown," she said in a low voice since she now stood less than two feet from me. "I tried ignoring it, but Spirit insisted."

I lifted my chin and stiffened. "I see." *No, I didn't.* Spirit never insists, only relays information. It's always been a medium's choice to act. Why is she really here?

"Your aura is showing some grey, are you ill?"

"If you have a message to deliver, please do so. I doubt you wish to be here anymore than I wish to see you."

She winced. "You haven't forgiven me yet. I understand."

I clenched my jaw, dropped my arms and stepped forward until we were nearly nose to nose.

"Forgiven? I should forgive the one person who convinced me to help find Timmy, only to abandon me to those vultures calling themselves reporters. I should forgive all of you who promised to stand by me, only to hide when I needed you most?" I stepped back, inhaled a sharp breath and turned away. "No, I haven't quite got to the point of forgiveness. If Spirit is insisting you come all this way to interrupt my new life, then so be it. What is the message?"

"Forgiveness is key," she raised her hand to stop me when I opened my mouth. "The message is that to take care as history is soon to repeat itself in a way which will allow you to accept forgiveness in yourself."

What? "What is that...no, don't answer. I'm assuming that is how you found me as well?"

"Yes. It was never my intention to disrupt your new life," she paused wrapping her bright colored purple shawl about her shoulders. "For that, I apologize. I will leave you alone now."

"Exactly as you left me before, not that I'm complaining. Good-bye Martha," I turned toward the counter and poured more hot water over my tea bag, clearly dismissing her. The sounds of her receding steps reached me, and I held my breath until the door opened, then closed. With shaking legs, I stopped and dropped into one of the chairs in our

little break room. Covering my face with my hands, I focused on evening out my breathing. A warm hand touched my shoulder.

"Are you okay?" Maggie asked.

I nodded without looking up. "I'm fine and please don't ask."

"I won't. Let me know if there's anything I can do."

I lifted one hand and tapped her fingers with my own. "I will. Thank you." I headed upstairs toward my bedroom.

Damn.

Chapter Six

I stretched out on my bed and stared at the ceiling, focusing on the small dim lights reflected there from the crystals. Calm. Harmony hopped up beside me, curling into my neck and purring softly. A cool breeze blew across my body.

"I'm here," Steph whispered beside me.

"I know," I kept my gaze on the ceiling. No need to look at her ghostly figure beside me. "I know I rarely, if ever ask you, but would you mind popping inside my head and let me flash through what happened a moment ago, so you'll know? I really don't think I can stand to say it out loud."

"Sure." Her voice whispered inside my mind, "Go ahead."

I let the time from when I first showed Maggie the ring belonging to Mitch's family flash through and ending when I walked upstairs to plop on my bed. The silence inside my head confirmed she'd left. I blanked my mind again and focused once more on the lights above me.

"I wish I knew who told her to deliver that message."

"Do you think that absolutely matters right now? I mean," I turned my head at this point to face her. "She's never misunderstood her messages."

"Neither have you."

I sighed. "No, only had them delayed."

"It's not an exact science, you know."

"Yep. Still, what do you think it means that history is going to repeat itself?"

"Not sure. But at least Maggie is willing to help you. Between her and everyone else you've told, I might not be much help anymore."

"Please don't say that."

"Hey," she said low.

"No. Not now, please."

"Okay. So, you found out a bit more about Mitch."

"Yeah, bit is right. Not enough, I don't think, that makes moving in with him a smart move."

"Then you know what you have to do. You gotta ask him."

"Uh-huh. I do."

"And you need to tell him more about your past too. Not only about Timmy and your gift, but including your box of trinkets. Also, what you've been doing with those items too."

"You're right."

"Ever wonder how come you can't see auras too?"

Sherrie Lea Morgan

I shook my head. "Nope. I don't want to see them either. That's a whole new realm I'm so not interested in learning."

Steph giggled, then spoke in a deep voice, "Your aura is very dark. Go to the light, Shan Anne."

I laughed. The light is what I needed right now. I rolled out of bed, bent and touched my toes before rising. Swiping my hair out of my face, I focused on Steph floating a few inches above my bed. "I'm done with that. Time for another vision with the ring." Stiffening my spine, I stomped to my office, slipped on my gloves, lifted the box of trinkets, and set it atop my desk. Lifting the lid, I searched for the ring and pulled it out. Removing my gloves, I lit the incense on my desk, on the shelves and punched the disc player sending soft peaceful notes floating around the room. Returning to my seat, I closed my lids and blanked my mind, focused on evening out my breathing and lifted the ring. Within minutes, an image formed in my mind of an older man standing inside Bobby's pawn shop talking to an older version of my neighbor. His grandfather. I'd recognized him from my earlier visions that I received on Bobby's own trinket I'd returned last year.

"Jack, are you sure? This isn't something to pawn without thinking about it long and hard," Mr. Green said holding the ring.

"Tim, I got no choice. Alessa's bills are coming in faster than I can pay them and the diner's at risk. I won't lose the diner, but I must pay these bills."

"Insurance isn't covering most of the costs?"

"You know them. Only pay what they absolutely have to."

"Still, this is one precious piece."

Tim slapped his hand on the counter. "Don't you think I know that? It's the only thing of value I have. Stop asking and give me what you can for it," he snapped.

"How much do you need?"

"You can't pay me that much. I'm not stupid and I won't take charity."

"Fine. Fine. Let me look this up in my book and see what I can do," Tim said.

"Thank you," Jack responded in a low voice and glanced around the store. "Can you hurry up, so no one sees me in here?"

"Sure thing," Tim said writing on a small paper and sliding it over the counter toward Jack. "This is what I can pay you."

After glancing at the paper, the man's shoulder's slumped. "I hadn't expected that much." He leaned in. "No charity."

Tim glared at him, "Charity isn't profitable."

Jack nodded. "I'll take it then."

Tim paid him and placed the ring in a small jewelry box. "I'll hold this in the back so you can come get it back once you're in the black."

Jack frowned. "I doubt I'll ever be able to afford it. Between the doctor bills and the diner, this is my last chance to save myself."

"You sure I can't spot you a loan? I got the money and we've known each other for years, I won't tell anyone, either."

"No," he shook his head adamantly. "No loans." He spun around and left.

Tim waited for him to leave before walking toward the back of his shop and slipped the ring into a large black bag hidden under a storage counter. He shook his head and returned to the counter.

The image faded out and another appeared of Jack sitting next to a hospital bed.

"Don't you worry about nothing, Alessa love. We'll be fine."

The woman frowned. "Don't lie to me, Jack Calabretti. You never could."

"I got the money to pay the bills and save the diner. We're not going to lose anything, I promise. You need to focus on getting better, my love."

A single tear escaped her eye and trailed down her cheek. "We both know that's not going to happen.

I've prepared myself for the inevitable. You need to, as well."

"I... I can't."

"It's getting closer to my time and I won't have you grieving so much you forget the children. You need to be strong for them."

"Please don't say that. I can't do this without you."

"You can and you will. Your stubbornness and will is one of the reasons I fell in love with you. We will be together again one day. Know that much and move forward. For me, love."

Jack dropped his head and whispered, "I will try for you."

The image faded out and I pressed a hand to my chest, rubbing against the ache inside. Returning the ring to the box, I rose and dropped onto the couch letting the cushions hug me. Tugging the lap quilt over me, I set my sight on the ceiling and reviewed the images I'd received. How strong they loved. Did all the men in Mitch's family love so deep? I let my mind drift to fantasies of Mitch declaring such a love for me.

Chapter Seven

Saturday morning, I squinted over the top of the quilt at Harmony who had chosen this moment to attack my feet. Luckily, I'd taken time to clip her sharp claws last night so she couldn't pierce the cloth and leave a blood trail across my ankles. My phone trilled and I stretched before grabbing the thing, seeing Mitch's name on the display. Hitting the button, I answered.

"Good morning, you," I whispered, crossing my fingers and ignoring the nervous twinges in my tummy.

"I finished the book," he said, and a hollow pit punched me in the gut.

"Good."

"I take it since you aren't the author, and you never mentioned having a child, you're the psychic mentioned in this thing?"

"I am."

"I guess I don't know you as well as I thought. We need to talk, then."

I closed my lids as a sour taste formed in my mouth. "Yes."

"I'll make plans to leave early this afternoon. I'd rather you come to my place, since it isn't out in the open and more private."

"Of course." Did he need a private place to end things? My body shuddered.

"Shoot me a message when you're on your way over. I'll make us some lunch. Can you get Maggie to cover the shop?"

"Yes."

"I'll see you then," he said and disconnected.

I dropped the phone on my chest and kept my lids closed wishing now I hadn't clipped Harmony's claws. Any pain she'd cause had to be less than this pain in my heart. He had no endearments for me. He had no sweet talk, nothing. I cringed when replaying our conversation in my head. His voice stretched across the line in a way I'd never heard it before. So flat and emotionless. *Move forward.* Apparently that's my new mantra for the new year.

Pressing my lips together, I escaped the warmth of my bed. New Year's resolutions need to be erased since it only seemed to bring more pain in my life than I had planned. I shuffled toward the bathroom to shower and dress for the day. Harmony meowed her displeasure of having to obviously wait to be fed. She'd live. I'd live. Standing under the spray of hot water, I let a few tears drop before forcibly shaking my body. *I'd live through this. I can do this. I will do this.*

****

Several hours later, after confirming with Maggie she'd cover my shift and close, I exited Trinkets and turned to walk up toward the intersection of Main and Storm. I paused before crossing and studied the dull gray light of the afternoon covering Cherished Heart Church and glinting off the stained-glass window set near the top of the front wall. The colors shown bright from the interior lights. I imagined the ghost Elaine haunting the tunnels beneath as Steph told me last July. Was she still there? Would she want to someday move on? I shrugged, turned and crossed the street. Walking past Main and past the small piece of grassy land which separated the diner and Mitch's home. Pausing at the walkway, I inhaled a deep breath and studied his family home. The soft moss green color of shingles lent an air of welcome, while the white shutters framing each window contrasted sharply against the darkened glass.

I grinned at the wrap around front porch. It'd be a perfect place to sit, drink iced tea and relax. His front yard spanned almost double the size of the house. The short white fence made me thing of his grandmother. How much had she worked on this

house to make it a home? How many generations of Calabretti's lived here before Mitch? I straightened my shoulders and headed toward the front door of solid oak with a delicate cut glass window. Knocking, I waited.

Mitch opened the door with a small frown. "Come on in," he said before spinning around and walking away.

No hug or kisses for me. Great. I followed closing the door behind me. In the kitchen, two settings with Porchetta sandwiches sat on the bar counter with sweating glasses of iced tea. He stood opposite the chairs and picked up his sandwich taking a bite, then waving to the chair for me to sit. I did. My stomach grumbled and I lifted the sandwich to my mouth. Even a small bite seemed like a large chunk of dusty week-old bread in my mouth. I grabbed a sip of tea to help wash it down. I placed my hands on my lap and faced him with raised brows.

"I'd assume you have questions for me?"

He dropped his sandwich and wiped his hands, nodding. "What do we both truly know about each other?"

"The events in that book happened shortly before I moved here."

"How long have you done those types of searches? Are you like, on some sort of list for the police or missing persons detectives to call?"

I shook my head. "No. there is no list that I know of. That search was my first and last."

"I guess with an outcome like you had, I don't blame you."

"I told you I was involved in the metaphysical culture. I believe in mediums, psychics, ghosts, tarot readings, the universe and Spirit."

He tipped his head to one side. "There's a big difference in believing in those things and actually participating in them."

I sat back. "It's like a religion. You can't believe and not interact." I leaned forward. "I mean, if you're a Christian, you pray, right? It's part of your belief system."

"I get that. I suppose I thought you only researched it or studied it," He lifted then dropped his hand. "I mean, I hadn't realized you practiced it in your life to that degree."

"Now that you know, do you have a problem with it?"

"Not with the idea of you living your life believing that way, or practicing it in your private ways." He pursed his lips.

"Private ways," I repeated.

He tapped his fingers on the table. "You know how I am about this. It shouldn't come as a surprise to you how I feel. Which is why I'm struggling with all of this coming as a surprise to me." He lifted his hand and fingered his hair. "I'm trying to understand here, as well as realizing how little we've talked about our pasts."

I blew out a quick breath. "In a sense, there's a lot we haven't talked about. I mean, why are you so determined to keep everything out of the purview of the gossipmongers. Which, I might add are everywhere and yes, more so in a small town. But, not nonexistent."

He winced. "I'm aware of that." He drank from his glass, then set it down before continuing. "You never talk about your parents. I know your grandmother raised you because they died. But you never told me how they died and never told me how you came to own Trinkets. It's not like it belonged to your grandmother. It belonged to her sister. How did you end up with it?"

"Aunt Caroline willed it to me because she didn't believe her own descendants would ever want it."

"Well, except when you first moved here. Her granddaughter, wasn't it? She wanted it."

"True. But like the attorney said, she waited too long to contest the will." My stomach growled again.

Drat it. I picked up the sandwich and took another bite. This time, it didn't feel like dust inside my mouth. I chewed and waited for Mitch to continue.

"It's hard to imagine growing up in different places since I've been here all my life. I'm glad, though. It's nice to know most everyone and it's almost like a very large extended family." He winked. "Not that we Calabretti's lack large families."

I blinked. Large families. Kids. My heart skipped a beat and I pressed my hand to my stomach. If he's mentioning kids, he's thinking long term. *Good.* I can work with this. Wait. Would he want kids someday? A bunch of them? Would they have a gift like mine? Please let there be a future for us. "Which I've only met a few."

"There's seven of us and bless my mom for still being sane with that many kids. Most of my siblings have moved to either the Carolina's or Florida. I guess I'm the only one who truly fell in love with Petrie's Crossing and never wanted to leave."

"None of your brothers or sisters felt the same at all?"

He shook his head. "Nope. When Mom and Dad decided to retire early, I got the diner. Of course, I grew up always wanting to own and run the place since I can remember. I've never regretted staying here and running it. I do have a lot of cousins around

here, since my mother's sisters live in Augusta. There's never a lack of family nearby."

"That's something I've never experienced." *I wish I could have that kind of support so close.*

"Some think it's suffocating, but not me," he paused, then continued. "So, this gift of yours..."

Would he and his family offer that kind of support to me? Did I need it? No, but I wanted it. Would he be willing to back me up like that? I cleared my throat. "It'll make a difference in how things are between us?"

Chapter Eight

"Honestly, I'm not sure yet. This is the first time I've felt I'm walking on uneven ground. If you could explain how this ability of yours works—"

"Psychometry," I said. "The ability is called psychometry."

"Okay, how does psychometry work, when did you develop it? Or have you had it since you were born?"

A flash of the day of my parents' accident entered my head and I quickly shoved it away. "I've had it ever since I was born. But, didn't truly understand what it was until later."

"Okay," he leaned back in his chair. "So, explain how it works."

Sucking in a quick breath, I answered. "First, let me explain that psychometry doesn't work the exact same way for everyone. For me, I get something like mini movie clips. Others only get colors, emotions or other ways that relay information," I paused and wiggled in my chair. "When I hold an object, I get those little clips. The good thing was that my Grandma Brenda believed me, unlike my parents.

She encouraged me to learn all I could about using my ability, since very few people have it at all. So, I did.

Right after high school, I got a job in a metaphysical store called New Day Metaphysical. Not only did they sell products used in the metaphysical culture, they also had a staff of mediums, channelers, psychics working to give private readings. One medium took me under her wing and helped me develop my ability. Her name was Martha Romana and she was a wonderful teacher. She invited me to join her when she did public, or rather group readings and events. My ability became well-known among the psychic community there." I glanced at my plate. I'd eaten everything already?

Mitch rose, taking out plates. "Let's get some wine and sit in the living room. It'll be more comfortable."

"Thanks," I said helping him, then grabbing my wine glass and following him into the living room. We both sat on the couch and I breathed a quiet sigh of relief when he draped his arm behind me. I took a sip of wine, then continued, "The year before the event you read about in that book, Martha and I did a class for forensic psychics."

"Forensic psychics?" Mitch asked.

I nodded. "Yes. It focused specifically on using one's psychic abilities to help with crimes."

He frowned.

"What?"

"From what I've read, I didn't think detectives put much stock in getting psychics to help with their cases."

"Some don't. A lot don't, to be honest. But there are some that do. Some are desperate enough to use anything or anyone they can to help solve cases. Especially cold cases, or missing persons... cases involving children are very sensitive."

"I don't doubt that. So how did you end up on this case?" He set his glass on the coffee table.

I inhaled deeply and set my wine glass aside, clasping my hands together. "The parents showed up at the shop where Martha and I worked. They were desperate for help. She introduced me to the parents, and I had my first vision. Together, we convinced the police we only wanted to help. Since a detective she'd been working on with other cases knew about her gift, he persuaded the locals to believe us. She talked them into giving me the lead."

"Why?"

I grimaced. "Because, my visions were clearer and contained more details than some of the other psychics working in that area of Birmingham." I lifted

my wine glass and stared into the dark red depths reflecting the dim light of the living room, then shook my head. "They convinced me I could help, so I agreed to work with them."

"Did the parents have a choice?"

"That's the thing. It was the parents who first told us of the case. They came in one day seeking help. Martha requested me back into the private reading room and had me do a reading on his stuffed elephant. I was able to see and relate the exact events of the day before he disappeared. This gave them hope and that's when they approached the detective and practically forced him to let Martha...or rather, me, in on the case."

"Okay, so everyone kind of pressured you into it?"

I tipped my head considering his question. "I can't say I was pressured, so to speak. It didn't take much to convince me to help. I truly believed I could find the boy. My training at that point, allowed me to minimize physical and emotional manifestations of my visions. To be honest, my confidence level during and before we found him, hit very high levels. There was no doubt in my mind, I'd find the boy within days." I glanced at my hands wringing in my lap. "And I succeeded. We located him in less than a week."

He placed his hand over mine. "I also heard the first forty-eight were the most critical in finding any child alive."

I nodded and focused on his tanned hand over my pale white fingers. A bitter laugh broke through my lips before I clamped them together. "My visions showed him alive all the way until the moment we located the wooded area where we found him."

"What?"

My head refused to lift. I couldn't face him. My voice dropped to a whisper, "He'd been killed only hours before we arrived." I swallowed past the lump in my throat. "It wasn't until we arrived at the tree where..." I waved my hand, "it wasn't until then that my last vision of him hit me."

Mitch scooted closer and placed his arms around me. "What was the vision?"

"His death."

Mitch gasped, dropped his arm and rose grabbing his glass. "I need more wine."

My shoulders dropped at his retreating back, and a slow burn began in my stomach making my lunch roil around in my gut. I rose and followed him. "That vision invoked emotions and physical manifestations I hadn't prepared for. I experienced his death, Mitch. Moment by agonizing moment."

He swung around and my jaw dropped at the paleness in his face.

"No one there knew what I went through. They only focused on the fact that the boy was dead and believed I had lied to everyone about him being alive." I turned my back toward him and continued. "There ended up being three major reactions. One, which included the police, who believed I used the case for fame and intentionally gave the parents false hope. The second group, the psychic community there determined I'd embarrassed them and incurred more disbelief of the abilities of the community." I inhaled deeply. "The third group, mainly people and reporters involved in missing cases believed I did a great job and wanted me to help them." I left my empty wine glass on the counter and returned to the living room to wait. After a few moments, Mitch joined me.

"The author did a great job keeping to the third group's belief's in his book," he said with a flat voice.

"Yes. The only problem is between the reporters and other people desperate for help in their own investigations nobody believed I had a right to privacy and hounded me nearly every day afterward. Even after Grandma Brenda passed, they didn't let up." I scowled at the pillow lying next to me. "They even invaded her funeral. I couldn't keep them away, so I packed my belongings and planned an escape."

"To here?"

I shook my head. "No, actually. I hadn't chosen a place when I met with Grandma Brenda's estate attorney. That's when I found out my Aunt Caroline existed and had willed Trinkets to my grandma, who in turn, willed it to me."

"You didn't even know about Caroline?"

"No."

"So, that's how you ended up here."

I nodded.

"It must have been quite the culture shock to go from living in a place as large as Birmingham to a small town like Petrie's."

I grinned. "It was an adjustment. But I don't regret a moment of living here."

"And what are you doing about your ability?" His eyes widened. "That's why you wear gloves at work."

"Yes, I can't take the chance of receiving visions while handling inventory."

"And Maggie hasn't guessed anything is up with that?"

Uh oh. "She did. Which is why I had her read the book before I gave it to you."

"I see."

Did he?

He shifted away from facing me and sipped his wine. "So, you told her before me. When did you tell her?"

I leaned forward and placed my hand on his forearm. "I only told her a few weeks ago because she tried giving me a recent purchase when I didn't have my gloves on, and I reacted badly. I needed to explain to her why I reacted the way I did."

"But she knew before me?"

"Yes."

I rubbed the ache in my chest. Please let him understand. Dang it. If he finds out who else knows about my gift and when they found out it could be disastrous for our relationship. No. Don't think about that now. Focus on the here and now.

"I didn't have a choice but to tell her before you because I was working up the courage to tell you," I whispered.

Chapter Nine

"Am I that scary?" He wrinkled his nose.

"You know you're not. But you have to understand that with your adamant stance about keeping things private, I'd be worried about your reaction."

"This certainly is a lot to take in, you understand."

"I do. And it is. But you also need to know how important you are to me in that I've revealed this to you." Was it so hard to understand that this wasn't easy for me either?

His brows rose. "What do you mean?"

"I didn't give Maggie all the details I gave you. She only read the book to understand my reasoning for wearing gloves." I told her much more about the items I've returned. How would he react with that information?

Mitch looked at the clock. "It's getting late. Let's hit the sack and continue this in the morning, okay?"

"Okay. I'm staying here tonight?" Butterflies took flight in my belly. Thank goodness.

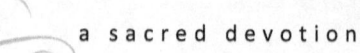

"Of course." He took my hand and we headed toward the bedroom. "There's a lot more I need to know to understand everything."

"What about the diner?"

"I'll text one of my cooks and have them open for me."

We prepared for bed and in the dark, I snuggled close to him. After I tell him the rest of my story, he might not want me here anymore. This could be my last night in his arms. His mossy scent surrounded me, allowing my muscles to relax for the first time in days, and I fell asleep quickly.

"Ms. Pryce, why did you let Timmy's parents believe he was still alive?"

"Ms. Pryce, what will you do now that your reputation is tarnished?"

"Ms. Pryce, why won't you help others?"

"Ms. Pryce, your co-workers claim you're a glory hound simply trying to make a name for yourself. What is your position?"

"Ms. Pryce, will you be assisting on any more investigations?"

Again, and again, the questions bombarded my ears so loudly, I barely heard the pastor speaking over Grandma Brenda's grave. He'd stopped twice to ask the reporters to have some dignity and to give me privacy. They ignored him, so he simply continued as though they weren't there. But they were. Steph tried tossing gusts of wind at them. But they refused to be deterred. The pounding in my head grew with the volume of their questions. I fell to the ground clamping my hands over my ears, tears streaming down my face and gulping for air with lungs which refused to cooperate. Please, please make them stop. A leg nudged my back while a hand grabbed my arm. I whipped around screaming at them to stop.

Timmy's fear filled face fractured any remaining hold I'd had on my emotions. No. No. I tugged at my hair searching for an external pain to erase the image in my mind.

"Nooo!"

"Babe, wake up," Mitch's voice pierced through the cacophony in my mind.

"I'm here. You're okay. Wake up," Steph's voice whispered in my mind and my body shivered with chills. I jerked around and forced my eyes open.

Mitch tugged the blankets over me. "It's okay, it's just a dream."

"Breathe," Steph whispered.

I nodded to both. "I'm awake," I croaked and curled into the warmth of Mitch's body. *"I'm okay now,"* I whispered inside my head to Steph. The temperature returned to normal. She'd left.

"Let me get you something to drink," Mitch said.

I grabbed his arms. "No, don't leave me. Please, stay here with me for a few more minutes." My heart raced and pounded against my chest.

"Do you want to talk about it?"

"It was the day of my grandma's funeral when the reporters broke in and tried to question me. They kept pushing so much, the pastor was forced to stop several times, and eventually I collapsed."

"I'm so sorry," he whispered kissing my temple while his hands rubbed my back.

I leaned into him soaking in the warmth of his body while I completed several breathing exercises to calm my body. Darkness surrounded us in his bed, so I closed my lids and focused on the sound of his heartbeat, the steady rhythm calmed my frayed emotions. *This.* This is what I want. We scooted under the sheets, wrapped in each other's arms and I forced my mind to blank. No dreams. Please no more dreams.

Chapter Ten

As Mitch fixed breakfast, I set the table and reflected on our talk from last night. I couldn't keep anything else from him. Move forward as I intend to continue. After we sat, I waited until most of the food disappeared from our plates, before speaking.

"There's more I need to tell you." There. Said it.

Mitch stiffened in his chair. "Okay, go on."

I took a deep breath. "When I inherited Trinkets, I obviously needed to clean the place and prepare for opening."

"Uh huh," he said.

Tucking my hands under my thighs, I continued, "I found a box of personal items not belonging to Aunt Caroline."

"What kind of items?"

"I call it my little box of trinkets. Jewelry, hair combs, watches, etc."

"And you're telling me this why?" Mitch asked frowning.

"Well, I also found Aunt Caroline's diary in the box and according to what she wrote, I gathered these

were items her lover used to ante when playing a card game with her."

"Oh yeah?" He laughed. "I thought you were going to tell me something else about your gift. I don't blame her. She was a lovely woman. No need for her to be alone."

"Well, that's the thing."

He tipped his head to the side. "What do you mean?

"I've been using my gift to return the items since I discovered most of them were pawned long ago, and Bobby's grandfather never put any up for sale. I think they were too important to let fall into the wrong hands. Although, I guess, him using them instead of poker chips is something to consider."

"You have?" His brows lifted. "How may have you returned?"

I lifted my hand and spread my fingers.

"Five?" He asked. "How?"

I dropped my hand. "I've been using my visions, searching for information in the diary and..." *Drat*. My heart pounded. Here's the hard part.

"And?"

I blurted, "And taking some people into confidence to explain how I figured they belonged to them."

He dropped his fork, letting it clatter on his plate and stared at me. He lifted one hand with its palm facing forward. "Wait a minute. You told me last night only Maggie and I knew about your ability."

"You and Maggie, the author and Marnie know about the events surrounding Timmy and the reason I moved here to escape."

He pinched the bridge of his nose and I could see the frustration settle into his features. "Explain, please."

"Some others...owners of the items I've returned know about my gift of psychometry." I spread my hands in surrender. "It was the only way to explain how I knew what I knew."

"I see." He cleared the table and dropped the dishes in the sink. I winced when it sounded as though a dish broke. He spun around crossing his arms across his chest and tipped his head to the side. "You're telling me two people know about all the details of your past and a lot more know about your gift...this gift of psychometry. Is that right?"

"Yes," I said.

He dropped his shoulders and his gaze. "You knew how much I cared for you when I made a room for you in my house and invited you to move in."

"Yes."

He lifted his gaze and frowned. "And not once did you consider that perhaps you should have revealed all of this to me?" He sucked in a large breath then released it. "I mean, I'm supposed to take your word you have this psychometry gift and the items." He ran his hands through his hair and then dragged them down his face before shifting his gaze away from me. "This is a lot to be dumping on me at this point in our relationship."

"I know." My stomach tightened.

He turned and faced the window with his back toward me, then lowered his head. "I'm not sure if I can ignore you keeping all of this from me for so long. It's been almost a year since you moved here and it's been nearly that long since we got together."

"I'm sorry." I bit my lip and rubbed my hand across my chest as the ache built inside.

"I don't know if that is enough right now. This is so much to take in." He shook his head and spoke over his shoulder. "I'm going to need some time to think about this. I don't know how much of what I'm feeling is simply anger or frustration."

"I understand." I rose, my legs shaky. "I'll go home, then."

"That's probably a good idea." He remained motionless.

I nodded at his back and left with my heart heavy inside. I couldn't blame him for reacting that way. It still hurt.

Chapter Eleven

I paused at his door with my hand on the knob. *Wait a minute.* Spinning around, I returned to the kitchen.

"I get that you need to think about all of this, but I'm trying to be honest here. I'm telling you these things because it's important to me you know about them. I had an idea it would cause a ripple between us, but I'm willing to take that chance, for you."

He dipped his head. "True. One concern," he raised a finger, "and my first of many is how did you plan to keep a lid on this? I mean, if you're helping everyone, and revealing your ability to them, you don't think they're going to talk about it?"

"I've asked them to not share and they've promised me."

"I'm sure they did. However, how many have you helped to a point where they can't keep it quiet any longer?" He blew out a breath and ran his fingers through his hair. "We can't ignore the fact that my roots are here. I grew up here. Everyone here knows me and, although they're getting to know you, Petrie's Crossing has been home to my family for

generations. Not yours." He crossed his arms again. "I'm not going anywhere. I can't. Not that I want to. I plan to grow old here and maybe, hopefully, raise my children here."

"I love it here. I don't want to leave here either." I protested hotly.

"You ran away from Birmingham because of that whole incident in the book. Your own people, so to speak, turned their backs on you and you left."

"So?"

"So, what will you do if it happens again?"

A wave of dizziness hit me while my heart raced making my hands shake while Martha's warning repeated itself in my mind. "I'm not doing that kind of work anymore. Ever again, so the chances of something similar happening is null," I said in a trembling voice.

"No one can predict the future. If it did happen, or something like it, then what?"

"What exactly are you asking me?"

"Will you run away again? You can as there isn't anything making you stay here."

"You."

"That's what I have to think about."

"I don't understand."

"You ran away once; you could do it again."

I gasped as my cold hand covered my throat. "You think I'll run away again?"

He shrugged, dropping his hands. "Can you say for certain you wouldn't?"

"I—"

"Don't answer that right now. Just think about it. I've lived through a public debacle. One that both embarrassed me and hit home hard enough to make even me consider relocating for a second. My roots and determination kept me here. A month ago, I might have believed the same of you. After what you've told me, I'm not so sure."

"Mitch, please." I begged.

"Think about what you're asking me to do. Not only accept everything you told me as the truth, which is a stretch, considering you've kept it from me from day one."

"But—"

"You've had plenty of opportunities to tell me before now. But you chose not to do so. It makes me wonder what else you might be keeping from me." He waved his hand in the air. "And it isn't only one thing, it's many things that could affect any future we might have had, or considered building together."

Past tense. Had. "Sounds like you've already made your decision," I accused him.

"No. I haven't. I'm just trying to get you to see my side of things."

Sure. My stomach clenched as I struggled to even my breaths and ran a hand through my hair, blinking then focusing on his face. Certain the hard thundering of my heart could be heard from where he stood across the room, I gritted my teeth then straightened my shoulders. "I guess I better leave so you can think about it. What I've told you took a lot from me to do. You might want to keep that in mind too."

"I will."

I spun around. *Perfect.* I bare my soul, and he wants time to think about it? Did I though? Had I been completely honest? *Drat.* I walked out of his home and took a long walk around the block before heading home. The cloudy sky prevented sunlight from filtering down darkening the day, which just so happened to match the darkness filling me inside. I blinked. No crying. Not now.

Chapter Twelve

Monday night, after closing the shop, I shuffled upstairs, fed Harmony and headed toward my office. Mitch hadn't called since I'd left his place after our breakfast discussion. Discussion, right. *Fight.* Lighting incense to ease the tension encapsulating my shoulders, I put on soft beach sounds and lounged on the couch staring at the ceiling.

"That bad?" Steph asked.

I squeezed my lids shut. "Worse."

"How so?"

"I feel raw inside. I told him everything."

"Everything?" She whispered softly, floating close to my side.

My face cooled as the blood drained away and I slid my glance around the room before returning to hers. *Drat.* "Nearly everything. It didn't help since he believes I've intentionally kept everything hidden from him." I sat up. "Rather than taking this revelation as a way for me to be closer to him and get him to understand me and what I went through and still go through, he's taking it all wrong."

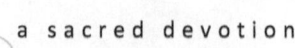

"Do you think he might believe your reveal might be a way to break things off with him?"

I gaped at her ghostly figure. "Why would he think that?"

She shrugged. "Just throwing things out here."

"I don't think that. It's more like his little world here in Petrie's Crossing is not as secure as he'd like it. I'm sure after whatever he endured with his ex-fiancée, my abilities and very public past is worse."

"Only if it's causes a public scandal, I'd think."

"He doesn't think I'd stay if something similar happens again. He thinks I'll run away like I did from Birmingham."

"But you wouldn't, right?"

"No. Yes. I don't know. And that's what scares me, probably more than him. I don't know if I'd run away again." I bit my lip. The thought that I'm not confident in my answer swirls around my mind. "No, I wouldn't. I mean, if we were together and he stood by me, I'd like to think I'd stay. That's the difference between here and Birmingham. I had no one there. If I had him, I'd stay."

"Something to consider..."

"What?" I asked.

"What if you lose him. Then would you consider running away again?"

"I don't want to lose him. I'm in love with him."

"Maybe you need to tell him that?"

"Maybe," I rose and stood near the desk. "Before I tell him anything, I need to return his family ring."

"You think that's a wise move considering what just happened over there?"

"With Mitch, I'm winging it here and I'm going to follow my heart. Wise or not, I need to return this before he stops speaking to me if it's what he chooses to do."

****

Wednesday morning, I squinted at the gray sky filtering through my windows. The weather matched the dimness in my mind along with the thousand elephants running rampant between my temples. My heart thudded dully against my chest. Tonight, I'd give Mitch his family ring or at least try to give it to him. I should have done this yesterday. But no, there had to be a big party at the diner with Mitch in the middle of it all. By the time that ended, I'd chickened out. Would he see me? I missed his evening goodnight calls these last few days. Poor Maggie tried her best to keep my spirits up with new shipments, great sales online, but although I could consider myself well off now, it didn't matter if I lost Mitch in the process. I rose and after showering and dressing for the day, sat in my office without the

lights on staring at my phone. Would he answer my calls? Should I call or wait for him to call? New Year's resolutions should be banned. They wreaked havoc in my life.

"Mornin'," Steph said floating over to the couch.

"Hey."

"Still no word?"

I shook my head. "Nope. I'm about to call him and see if he'll meet with me so I can give him the ring."

"You ready for whatever happens?"

"It's been over a day and a half since we've talked." I let out a long exhalation while giving her a half-hearted shrug. "I'm tired of being in limbo. I might as well get this done. Then there's only one thing left before I completely back off and let him figure out what he wants to do."

"One more thing besides the ring?" Steph asked.

"Yeah." She isn't going to like what I decided to do last night.

"What is it?"

"Not yet. I'll explain when I'm ready to do it, ok?"

"I can always peek, you know."

"Yes, you can, but you won't, because you promised me you wouldn't."

"True," she said rising and floating near the window. "Call if you need me, okay?"

"Absolutely," I said, and she faded out. Pressing my lips together, I punched my phone to call Mitch.

"I'm pretty busy here. Got a large group coming in tonight."

"I'll make it quick. I have something I need to give you. Can you come over after you close up?"

Silence. I crossed my fingers.

"I don't know how late I'll be."

"I'll be awake," I rushed on. "You don't have to stay afterward. No expectations."

His sigh echoed across the line. "This can't wait?"

"No." Yes. *Ugh.* No.

"I'll see you later, then."

"Thank y—." He'd disconnected without another word, and a sharp stab shot through my chest. *Damn.*

Chapter Thirteen

Later that evening, I lit every calming incense aroma I could in my office, set my music to a low mediation melody, and set out my trinket box. Sliding on my gloves, I lifted out the gold ring with the monogrammed letter C on the front and studied it. The visions I'd had along with the information from Aunt Caroline's diary drew a clear picture. How to explain all of this to Mitch? Would it matter? It had to on some level. I set the ring on the cloth I'd laid out in the center of my desk and leaned back, letting my eyelids close.

Focusing on my breathing, I inhaled slowly and released each breath slowly, letting my body relax. I kept my mind blank preventing any visions from arriving and disrupting my meditation. Be focused and clear. Mitch's words floated in and I let them bounce around in my mind for a moment. Honesty and openness are required here.

Mitch finally arrived around eleven and I led him to my office. No welcoming kiss, hug or smile. *Well, it is what it is, I suppose.* As we entered the office, I waved a hand toward the couch.

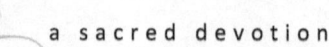

"If you'll have a seat, I have something to give you," I said heading toward my desk and slipping on my gloves. Thankfully, I'd replaced the box in the drawer before. I lifted the ring and joined him on the couch, holding out my hand toward him. I opened my fingers, revealing what I held.

He gasped and took the ring, holding it in his clasped hands, frowning. "How did you get this?"

"It was in my box I told you about."

"But, how? I mean, why?" He twisted in his seat, rolling the ring around in his palm. "You did your thing with this item too?"

"Yes." I swallowed. "Do you want to know what I learned?"

He opened his hand and stared at the ring for a moment before slipping it into his shirt pocket, then faced me. "Go ahead and tell me what kind of visions you had."

I tried to smile and failed miserably. "Sometimes, the visions I get explain how the item got into Aunt Caroline's possession. Sometimes, they come with visions of where they've been, so to speak." I paused.

"Go on," he said.

"The visions, along with some searching through Aunt Caroline's diary, tell me that your grandfather pawned this ring for money to cover your grandmother's hospital bills along with keeping the payments current on the diner."

"There was never a problem with the diner. I don't remember ever hearing anything about my grandfather having money problems," he crossed his arms. "In fact, I'm sure I would have heard about it when this ring disappeared."

"What do you mean?"

"This ring was promised to me when I turned eighteen and decided I'd take over the diner one day. Dad never cared for wearing jewelry. My grandfather told us, my dad and I, that it had been stolen."

My jaw dropped for a second before I closed my mouth and considered what he'd said. "My visions show your grandfather sitting next to your grandmother while she was in the hospital. They also showed me him pawning the ring and making Bobby's grandfather promise never to tell anyone." I lifted, then dropped my hand. "Perhaps that is how he got enough money that no one would be suspicious. If he pawned it, he'd have that money and any insurance money from it being reported as stolen."

Mitch stood abruptly. "My grandfather would never commit insurance fraud."

I rose. "I'm not saying he would. Did he claim it?"

Mitch shrugged. "I honestly don't know, and I don't care. But your visions aren't accurate because my grandfather never had any financial issues. In fact, I remember him helping me open my first savings account and teaching me how to manage money. I learned math by helping my dad with the books at the diner."

"I can only interpret my visions based on what I see. How old were you when your grandmother passed?"

"Why does that matter?"

"Maybe your parents didn't want you to know?"

"When I took over the diner, I took over everything. Don't you think I'd have known if it was ever in any kind of dire financial situation?"

"Not if he kept the bills paid on time, you wouldn't."

"I don't know about this." He rubbed his hands over his face.

"This? You mean my visions? I only get what the items show me. There's no reason for them to show me something false. I'm not lying." How dare he question my gift?

"I'm not saying your vision is false. I'm saying I think you might have interpreted the vision incorrectly. No one is infallible."

"No, they aren't. But I've been doing this my whole life and never misinterpreted a vision."

"Even with the missing boy?" Mitch asked.

A lead weight dropped into the pit of my stomach making me cringe. "My visions were not interpreted incorrectly during that search. Every vision I had showed him alive." How could he even say that? "It wasn't until the end...I explained that to you."

"I know, I know." He lifted his hands palms up. "I'm just saying what you're telling me doesn't make sense." He strode toward the window and stared out into the dark night. "I'll have a talk with my parents. See if they knew anything about this."

"Fine. Double check it all."

"Do you understand why I feel like I have to, right? "

"I do. You don't trust what I'm saying. You're doubting what I've told you and you have every right to verify its validity. That's your right as the owner of that ring. So, now that I've returned it to you, my part is done with it."

Mitch turned. "Thank you for returning the ring."

"You're welcome."

"It's one more thing to add to everything I've learned about you so far. I'm still struggling with the fact that it seems like I'm the last one in town to

know about." he waved his hand to encompass the office, "all of this and your past."

I clenched my jaw. "You're not the last. I told you only a few know and that's because I returned items to them, or they found out."

"I wasn't the first or the second. I wasn't even the third person to know," he said.

"I've apologized for that. I told you why things had to go the way they did."

"I know that. I'm just trying to get you to see things from my point of view."

"I get it. Trust me, I get everything you're saying," I snapped.

He stiffened at my quick defensive response, dipped his chin and left. Fine. Leave. Drat that man and my New Year's resolutions. Drat this gift of mine. Blowing out a breath, I flopped onto the couch. Drat everything. I lay there in the softly illuminated office for a few minutes, before I eventually rose, turned off the lights, and headed to bed. Alone.

****

Thursday morning, I met Maggie when she arrived to open the store. Her clothes slightly wrinkled, matching the dark rings under her eyes. "You okay?" I asked.

"Not really. I'm having a hard time finding a place close to Main to live. I want to be right here, but there's nothing readily available." She shrugged. "I'll figure it out."

"I'm sure something will come open for you."

"Yeah, I'll cross my fingers," she tipped her head to the side. "How are you doing?"

Shrugging, I tossed her a small smile. "Not good either. Seems like we're in the same boat as far as our luck is concerned."

"You haven't worked things out with Mitch, yet?"

"I gave him the ring that belongs to his family last night. He wasn't happy about what I revealed to him from my visions. In fact, he's still having an issue with finding out about me, my gift and past, and the fact that there were others who knew about it before he did."

"But, that's not your fault. You were helping people before things got serious with him, so he can't expect that you'd tell him all about this like on your second date. Men," she said with a huff. "such a pain in the butt. He'll come around though. He's such a great guy, I'm sure he'll work it out inside his head and be okay."

I lifted my brows at her. "You actually think so?"

"You love him?"

"I believe I do," I said nodding my head.

"Then don't give up. Give him some time to take everything in and realize how much he loves you too."

"See that's the thing," I said.

"What?"

"He hasn't come out and said he loves me."

She chuckled and placed an arm around my shoulders before lowering her voice. "Shannon, Mitch is not the type of man to ask just anyone to move in with him. If he did that, he loves you or is super darn close to it. That's a big commitment from someone who likes things to be kept private."

"That's the thing, though. He likes to have things private, but he's living in a small town where nothing is private. Don't you think his expectations are too high?"

She shook her head. "Nope. I agree living in Petrie's makes keeping things private hard, but not impossible. I mean, look what all you're learning about everyone as you return those items. It's not like everyone's life here is posted in the local paper or anything."

"It's talked about."

"Yeah, but quietly. Not out for strangers to see." She turned on the computer. "Think about that. Gossip yes, public yapping, no." She headed toward the break room and I followed her. "Don't give up on him yet, okay?"

"I won't."

"Good. Now, let's have some tea and see if anyone wants to shop today."

As I helped her prepare the tea, I couldn't stop thinking about what she'd said. Did he actually love me?

Chapter Fourteen

Sunday morning, I crossed the street heading for the diner. Mitch hadn't made any attempts at contacting me since Wednesday night. What was going on? Kim, the server met me when I entered the patio dining area and waved to the empty table near the side.

"Go ahead and grab a seat, I'll be right with you," she said before reentering the diner. A few minutes later, she bustled out, served the couple sitting three tables away before joining me. "What can I get you?"

"I'll have what I always have, but can the eggs be scrambled this time, please?"

"Absolutely," she said then turned.

I touched her elbow and lowered my voice. "Is Mitch here?"

She frowned. "No, sorry. He left to visit his parents in Florida Thursday morning and said he'd be gone for a few days."

"Who's cooking?"

"Oh, Ms. Michelline's son arrived in town two weeks ago and Mitch hired him on as one of the

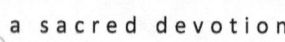

chefs," she grinned before continuing. "His name's Zach and he's doing a great job. You'll love his food."

"Sure thing." She left to turn in my order. Mitch left town without saying anything. No call? My shoulders slumped as I stared at my hands clasped in my lap.

"Since you've been missing our tea dates, I haven't had a chance to visit with you in ages. May I join you?" Ms. Michelline asked.

My head jerked and I nodded. "Of course. I'm so sorry about missing tea. I've been a bit busy lately and got completely sidetracked."

"That's alright sugah," she said leaning forward. "My son has come home." She grinned leaning back. "I'm so happy Mitch is giving him a chance to cook here. His creole recipes are mighty fine."

"Oh?" I asked.

"He used to cook in one of those fancy restaurants in Nawlins," she winked. "I'm hoping Mitch will let him put a few of his dishes on the menu. I do so miss good creole cuisine."

"So, he moved back to live here for good, then?"

She frowned. "Yes. Why wouldn't he?"

I lifted my palms up. "Just asking. Is something wrong?"

She shook her head. "No. I was simply wondering if you'd had any idea if this might be a good or bad move?"

"Oh no. Nothing like that. Small talk only and curiosity."

"Ah yes. Well, if you come to tea on Monday, I'll explain where he's been."

Where he's been? "Sure. I won't miss it, I promise."

We ate our breakfast and chatted about our holidays. I tried focusing on the conversation, but Mitch's sudden departure kept intruding on my thoughts.

"I'm sorry?" I asked when I caught her staring at me.

"I asked how Maggie was working out. I heard her grandmother is finally near the top of the list for getting into that special housing over in Augusta."

"She's still looking for a place close to Main. Nothing much available right now."

"She'll find something."

I smiled. "That's what I told her." After breakfast, I hugged her good-bye and paid my check, then walked back to Trinkets. Yes. Mitch had a lot to think about. Yes, we had our discussions and I promised to give him time to consider everything. But we were still a couple. Or so I thought. So, why did he leave town and not at least let me know? I wouldn't leave without saying anything. I checked the time when I got back to the store. A couple more hours still left before I needed to take over the counter. Good. I rushed to my office, got comfortable on the couch and called Mitch. He answered after three rings. Without waiting for a greeting, I plunged in.

"You didn't think to let me know you were going out of town?"

"I told you I needed time to think. My father called and needed some help unloading some building materials his friend gave him, so I'm doing both here."

"It's one thing asking for space. It's another leaving town without notice."

"I have everything covered at the diner. I didn't realize I needed to get your permission."

Oh heck no. Attitude won't work on this. "As your girlfriend slash lover who you asked to move in with you, I assumed I had a right to know if you up and decide to leave town. I'd do the same for you. Am I wrong?"

His quick breath echoed in my ear. "Would you?"

"What does that mean?"

"It means, if something were to blow up regarding your secrets, would you tell me before you tucked tail and ran?"

"How could you ask me that? I'm not the one who just left town." Hypocritical jerk. "Why would you ask me something like that?"

"It's happened to me before."

"Who? Your ex-fiancée left town without telling you? Is that what happened? Because, I don't know what happened. You never talk about it and since this is all about trusting each other, that should be something I should know about, don't you think?" I rubbed the back of my neck. Why am I arguing with him on the phone?

"It's in the past and has nothing to do with us."

What? "Doesn't it? I mean consider this." I waved my hand while I paced. "You're upset about my secrets, sure. But you're more upset about how public they can become. Publicity is something you don't like. Why? Have you been like that since you were little? I doubt it affected you that much. I bet it's because of your ex-fiancée, so yes, it has something to do with us. Since I've told you everything," I grimaced. Except about Steph. "I think it's only fair for you do the same."

"On the phone?" He asked.

"Might as well." Especially since he obviously can't face me.

His sigh carried over the line. "We met in Atlanta when I was doing an internship at one of the hotels.

She moved to Augusta not long after we met to be closer."

"Why not relocate here?"

"There wasn't any work here for realtors which is what she did."

"Okay." That made sense...sort of.

"After six months, she decided Augusta was too small to live in. But she'd put up with it because she wanted to marry me. It wasn't until another two months passed, when she realized I would never leave Petrie's Crossing. She told me she wasn't sure if she could live in such a small town as she craved the excitement and fast pace of big city life. She had no problem being very vocal of how small Petrie's was, how disappointed in the lack of nightlife and clubs. She consistently teased my staff of lying stagnant in a hole-in-the-wall town. She left without a word, ended up mailing my ring back to me. There, that's the whole story."

"And everyone knows but me, right?"

I pulled the phone away to stare at it for a second, before placing it back to my ear. "You're honestly throwing my words back at me?"

"Darn straight I am. Listen, there's no such thing as privacy in a town this small. Everyone knows practically everything about everyone who lives here."

"True, but not everyone publicizes everything either."

"I haven't publicized anything."

"Not directly. Privacy doesn't guarantee secrecy. Gossiping goes hand in hand here."

"I agree. However, since the items I've returned and the people who know about my gift have given me their word on keeping my secret, specifically because the items I've returned have made an invaluable impact in their lives. That is worth something to them."

"And the more items you return, the more people will know. Before you or I can stop it, it'll become general knowledge here."

Was that really what he worried about? *Don't give in.*

Chapter Fifteen

"So what? No one has ostracized me yet. I don't think anyone will. Will you?"

"All I'm saying is keeping your gift, ability, whatever on the down low will be nearly impossible."

"I disagree." I stopped and leaned against the wall, staring at the ceiling. I hated arguing.

"How can you?"

"Because I've been returning items since the month I moved here, and you first found out about any of this when I told you. Had anyone mentioned anything to you before? You catch any gossip about me other than when I messed up returning some items? No, you haven't. There are plenty of people in this town. Your town. My town, that know how to keep a secret and a promise. Keeping their word means something to them."

"Are you accusing me of not being able to do the same? It's not that as much as you've lied to me by omission. It's almost as bad."

"Stop being an ass. You know I'm not saying you can't keep a secret. And I haven't lied by omission.

There wasn't any reason to tell you until now. That's all I'm saying."

Silence.

"Is it?" He asked.

What did he mean by that? I stiffened as my hand tightened on the phone. How dare he. *That's it.* "You know what? While you're down there, think about what I said. It's taken nearly ten months for you to find out about me and only because I told you. No one else did. Think about that while you're considering everything else." *Damn him.* I squeezed my lids to keep the tears from falling and bit my lip. I lowered my voice. "Consider that along with what I've been through and, again, how difficult it was to share everything about me, while you're busy figuring out what you want by putting space between us." I sucked in a deep breath and pushed on. "My gift is very precious to me. I won't deny that or what it has helped me do since I moved here. I can't stop helping people. I won't. If you think I will, you're wrong. And that's something I guess I need to think about."

"Maybe there's too many hurdles for us to jump here to make this work."

My jaw clenched. "I guess you're going to have to decide if I'm worth it...and vice versa. I'll talk to you later," I said disconnecting the call. *There.* I sighed.

Yeah, there. I told him. If things got bad, would he stand beside me? Help me, protect me or push me away to avoid being in the limelight?

I paced letting our conversation replay in my head. No. I won't stop helping people regardless of how things progress or stop between us. A gift is called that for a reason, that's what Martha taught me. It's helped more people than not. I slumped. Except me. It hasn't helped me. It's only caused me pain. Curse or gift? Help others while I suffer? That's not fair. The faces of the ones I've helped flash through my mind. Their gratefulness, their tears, their happiness did make me feel good. It's a gift and I'm sticking to that.

"You okay?" Steph whispered in my mind. "Do you need me with you?"

"I'm having a little pity party right now."

"So, you're fine. Call if you need me."

I snorted. "Love you," I whispered back in my mind.

"Always," she responded.

"Always," I repeated.

And it would be always. That much I knew. *Remember that.*

Chapter Sixteen

After closing shop on Sunday, I headed upstairs into my office. Sitting behind the desk, I studied my small office with its incense holders sitting about, the candles surrounded by stones I'd set out and frowned. Booting up the computer, I focused on balancing the books for the business, ignoring the nagging questions plaguing and crowding inside my mind all weekend. My screen flickered causing me to glance toward the couch. Steph's misty white form solidified into a more solid shape sitting on the arm of the couch.

"How're you doing?" She asked.

I lifted then dropped one shoulder, refocusing on the job at hand. "Working."

"Hear from him since your last chat?"

"Nope," I said and sat back in the chair. "What do you think about the idea of me telling him about you?"

Her ghostly shape shimmered before solidifying. "No."

"No?"

"Haven't you told him enough?" She floated over near the edge of the desk. "I mean, you've already given him a boatload of information to consider. If you go to him with one more thing, it might be too much."

"Part of me keeps thinking we should have full disclosure."

"You're not marrying him. And even if you were, do you truly think telling him you converse with your dead twin sister's ghost is going to help make matters better?"

I pursed my lips. "After everything else, it might not be so bad."

"Yes, it would. Think about it," she floated in a pacing movement between the desk and couch. "Singletons can't understand twins completely. Never have, never will. No matter how many times we've tried to explain, they don't get it. They can't. How can they understand when one twin is dead, and the other is alive? You think it'd be easier?"

"Sometimes they get it. Especially when we explain it's like being married."

"No, they don't. Get real. They think they can, but unless they're a twin themselves, they don't. Even other twins who aren't close don't get it. Only those who have the same close tie with each other understand."

"Does that make sense to you? How come all twins aren't like the close ones?"

"Don't know. Don't think about it."

"Either way, I think it's important to tell Mitch. If I put everything on the table, then if or when he wants to continue or move forward in our relationship, then he'll know everything."

"You're acting desperate."

I jumped to my feet. "What are you talking about?"

"Listen, it's not like he's asked you to marry him, right?"

"So?"

"So, you've never told anyone, not even Martha about me. Why him? Besides...it's not like this will last forever."

"This? What this are you talking about?"

"Neither one of us know how long I can stay here with you. Neither of us know why I was able to stay to begin with, other than it had something to do with how close we are. Not every close twin's ghost hangs around, you know."

"What?"

"What if once you and Mitch make up—"

"If we make up."

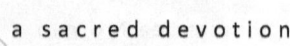

"When that happens, you'll have someone with you who loves you and will take care of you. Someone alive. It might be the time for me to go."

"Don't say that."

"You might not need me around."

"I'll always need you."

"No, you won't and stop panicking. I'm just saying it might happen."

"I can't lose you."

"Yes, you can, if you have Mitch."

"No, I don't think even he can help me like you do."

"Don't start crying. It's a possibility we both must face, is all I'm saying. And when it happens...if it happens, there won't be a need to tell him about something that is no longer happening, right?"

I glared at her through the mistiness in my eyes. "You're not making any sense."

"Fine. Forget I said anything about me leaving. It doesn't matter right now, because it's not happening. The main point is that you can't tell him about me. You can't tell anyone about me. Ever."

"What if I decide I want to?"

"You'd have to prove it, right? I mean, I'll make sure no one hears me or sees me. You'll look like you're crazy. You want to try that?"

"You'd really do that to me?"

"Yes."

"You'd intentionally let me look crazy after all this time?"

"You can't ever tell anyone about me."

"Clara knows. She's seen you."

"She's a kid. Most kids see ghosts anyway. Their parents all think it's imaginary friends, so she wouldn't be taken seriously."

I dropped in my chair. "I can't believe you'd legitimately do that to me."

"Only if you push it. Have I ever asked anything of you? I mean, for myself. No. So get over it. This is one rule I won't budge on. I mean it."

"Obviously."

"It's not fair to me for you to tell anyone for your own selfish reasons."

I gasped. "Selfish reasons?"

"Stop repeating me."

I waved my hand in dismissal. "I won't tell him or anyone. Happy?"

"No. But satisfied."

I frowned. "Well, that's good. I guess."

"Listen. If he chooses to break things off with you, it's not the end of the world. You weren't looking for any kind of relationship when you moved here in the first place."

"True. But, I'm in love with him now. I don't want to lose him."

"Good. But, how far are you going to take this? Have you told him how you feel? You need to know how he feels too. Has he told you he loves you?"

"No. But I know he cares a lot for me if he's asking me to live with him."

"Please think about this whole thing. If it's worth it, fight for him. If not, let him go and move on."

I stared at her flickering image. "What's going on?"

"What do you mean?" Steph asked.

"You've been acting weird for the last couple months."

"You're imagining things," she said and faded out.

No.   No,   I'm   not.

Chapter Seventeen

Two days later after I'd rose and fed Harmony, the bell over the front door of Trinkets rang announcing Maggie had arrived to open for the day. Sitting at the small counter in my upstairs kitchen, I munched on a piece of toast and counted the days since I'd seen or heard from Mitch. It'd been a week since our last face-to-face meeting and over three days since I'd spoken to him on the phone. I spotted him across the street yesterday, but had no idea when he returned to town. He hadn't called or tried to see me, which was fine as I had a lot of thinking to do about where our relationship seemed to be heading myself.

I let out a long breath and sipped my tea. All this turmoil started with my darn New Year's resolution. At least, I wasn't keeping any more secrets from him. Except Steph. Well, that was one to take with me to the grave, I suppose. No sense rocking the boat more than I already had with that little tidbit. One way or the other, the man needed to decide. Things can't go on like this too much longer.

"Shannon?" Maggie called up.

"Be right there," I said, tossing the last half of my toast into the trash and making my way downstairs.

Maggie stood near the cash register with her hands shoved deep in her pockets. As I approached, she tried to smile, but it didn't last very long. I tipped my head to the side and raised a brow.

"What's up?"

"My grandmother got the call."

The call? "That's good news, isn't it? I mean, I even checked out that assisted living place myself. I think she'll love it there."

"She will. I know. It's only…" She trailed off.

"Don't worry about finding a place to live. I'm sure there's something around here. You might have to look farther out, though than right here on Main Street."

"I don't have much time."

"What do you mean?"

"I need the rest of this week off to relocate and get Grandma settled in her new place," she blew out a quick breath, then continued, "Then I need to get the house packed and cleaned. The landlords were notified along with my grandmother, so they know she's moving. They've given me two weeks from tomorrow to move out."

"Two weeks? Are you kidding me? That's not fair."

"It wouldn't be if I were on the lease with my grandma, but I'm not. As far as they're concerned, once she moves out, it's considered vacant."

"Well, shoot."

"Shoot is right. I even tried having a realtor help me, but the only place reasonably close is outside of Augusta. I don't want to live that far away. I love Petrie's and genuinely hoped I could live here."

"I have an idea," I said. "Let me call Bobby. He knows everyone around here and perhaps someone might have a room you can rent temporarily until you find a place?"

"I could do that."

I tugged out my phone and punched in Bobby's number. After explaining the situation, he gave me an address. I wrote it down, thanked him and grinned at Maggie. "He says this place is for rent and it's only a few houses down from Mitch's place."

"That's not a bad neighborhood."

I checked the time. "Let's go check it out now, since it isn't like we have a bunch of customers in here."

"You sure?" She asked.

"Of course. Come on," I said, and she grabbed her purse following me outside. I waited for her to lock up, then we both turned and headed up the street to

the crosswalk. "Mitch's house is practically behind his diner, so you should be within walking distance."

"How are we going to get in? I mean, don't we have to call first to let someone know we want to check it out?"

"Bobby says they're doing a bit of renovation work this morning and he knows the contractor on site. He's going to call him, It's Greg something, and let him know we're coming over and he'll let us inside to look around."

"That's great." Maggie lifted her hand to show her fingers crossed. "I hope this works out."

"Me too."

The morning grey clouds filled the sky...again. Spring can't get here soon enough. I miss my moments in the sun. Sighing, Mitch's face popped in my mind. Stop thinking about him. *Right now, I should focus on helping Maggie.* The cool air closed around us making me rub my arms. I should've worn a jacket. I slid a glance at Maggie, noting she still wore her coat. She hadn't removed it before telling me the news. We walked past Mitch's place and I kept my eyes averted. The hammering of tools resounded a house down from our destination.

"At least the owner is getting it fixed some before trying to rent it."

"Yeah. Let's hope it doesn't require a lot of work."

"Agreed."

Once we arrived, I asked one of the workers for Greg. We were directed into the house where the sounds of men grunting echoed. Making our way carefully over the piles of ripped out carpet, we made our way into what appeared to be the living room. Three men appeared to be struggling to maneuver a dented stove strapped to a dolly through the doorway between the kitchen and living area. Black streaks marked the faded painted walls of the hallway leading down to several doors. Bedrooms and bathroom, probably. One man from the group, let the other two take the stove out and turned to face us.

"You Maggie and Shannon?"

We nodded. "Bobby call you?" I asked.

"Yep," he said waving his arm to indicate the living room. "It's a mess here. We only started demo work this morning and it's been vacant for a week already." He frowned. "The last tenants had several dogs they didn't care to keep very clean and we had to have pest control out here to get rid of the fleas."

My shoulders slumped when I glanced at the large ceiling stain. "Roof leaks too?"

"Yeah. Bobby said you were looking for a place. But I'll be honest with you. The clean-up work alone is gonna take another month after which we gotta come back in and paint, put new carpet in, install a new sink and that doesn't include redoing the whole hall bathroom. Looks like the previous tenants let their dogs live there the whole time they were here. Everything from the floor to cabinet is chewed up. The toilet is broken, and the tub is cracked."

"Oh wow," Maggie said.

"Well, thank you for letting us in," I said and laid a hand on Maggie's shoulders. "We'll get out of your way."

"Sure thing," he said before returning to the kitchen.

Neither of us said anything until we arrived at the sidewalk and had walked past the neighbor's place.

"What an awful mess. There's no way I can wait for them to get that place cleaned up."

"I know. I'm sorry."

"It's not your fault," Maggie said.

I looked ahead and froze. Mitch stood on the sidewalk setting his trash bins along the curb. His face seemed dark and it looked as though he hadn't shaved in a week. Wrinkled clothes hung on his body. I'd never seen him look so disheveled and bit my lip to keep from calling out to him. He must have sensed us as his head jerked up. His eyes widened as he took a step toward us, only to stop and tuck his hands in his loose jeans' pockets.

"Go on and talk to the poor man," Maggie whispered beside me. "I'll cross the street here and get back to the store."

I nodded without saying anything, then walked toward the man of my dreams and current source of heartache. I stopped in front of him, gazing into those chocolate colored eyes. My body yearned to be next to his and I clenched my hands together to keep from reaching for him.

"Hi," I said.

"Where were you coming from?" He asked.

I glanced over my shoulder then back to him. "Maggie and I went to check out a house for her to rent. But it won't be ready for a few months and she needs to find a place soon. Her grandmother is moving into an assisted living place this weekend. Maggie only has two weeks to pack the house and move out." I was rambling, but couldn't stop. "So, I called Bobby and he told us about the house down the street. But, it's in bad shape. I was thinking about calling Marnie since she has that huge house all to herself. I'm sure she'd be okay renting a room out to Maggie, don't you think?"

He nodded. "I bet she would."

"That's what I was thinking. That way, Maggie could still be close to Main Street like she wanted and within walking distance of Trinkets." I sucked in a

breath and pushed on. "When did you get back in town? How are your parents? Did you get that stuff done you went to help with?"

He tipped his head to the side.

"You could have called," I said. *Say something.*

"I know."

That's it? I swallowed past the lump in my throat and shifted my gaze past him. A small group of tourists snapping pictures headed our way. "There's some people coming this way."

Mitch glanced behind him, before turning toward his house. Would he invite me in? I waited, holding my breath. His sigh carried over to me.

"I gotta go. I'm due in at the diner this morning," he said walking away.

So, no invitation to come in and talk. I guess that's all the answer I needed. I blinked away the moisture building in my eyes and ran across the street without looking. Luckily, no one was coming, and I made it across safe. Letting the tears fall, I stared at the ground making my way back to the store. Drat the man.

Chapter Eighteen

Friday evening as I closed shop, Nancy strode through the front door of Trinkets.

"You have to do something," she said.

"What are you talking about?" I asked moving behind her. "I'm closing for the day, so unless you want to leave through the back door, you'll have to go out now."

"Go ahead and lock up. I'm talking about Mitch. The staff is complaining about his condition."

"Condition?" What on earth was she talking about?

"He's been snapping at the staff, coming into work looking like he hasn't slept in days...he's growing a beard for heaven's sake!"

"And that's my responsibility how?" I asked, dreading her response.

"Listen, I know something is going on between you two. It doesn't take a genius to figure out you two have had a spat or something. But it needs to end. He looks horrible."

"Again, why is that my fault? Or better yet, why are you assuming it's my fault?"

"You saying you have nothing to do with the fact that he looks like he's lost weight, he's grouchy and not at all like his normal self? I mean, even when his ex-fiancée called off the wedding, he didn't look this bad."

I glared at her until she planted her hands on her hips and glared back.

I shrugged. "We're having an issue that we're working out between us, okay?"

"What's the issue?"

"None of your business to begin with. Second, it's more of him having the issue rather than me."

"You tell him it's over?"

"No, I didn't."

She crossed her arms. "Then what's going on?"

I lifted my hands, then let them drop. "It's his thing to work out."

"But, he's miserable. Everyone can see it."

"It's not my fault." Yes, it is. "I mean, not all my fault. He hasn't spoken to me in days. I didn't even know he went out of town or when he got back. I can't control what he does or how he feels."

She dropped her hands. "How do you feel? Because, to be honest, you're not looking so great yourself."

"I've been trying to give him space. He's taking time to figure some things out, that's all."

"I don't get it."

"Not everything is as it appears. No matter what you might think."

She hugged me. "I thought we were friends by now," she whispered in my ear.

I blinked away the tears threatening in my eyes. "We are," I said hugging her back. "I'm fairly sure I can make things better. There're some things I told him that he's having a hard time dealing with. That's all I can say."

She leaned back and peered at me. "You tell him you love him?"

"No, it's not that."

"Maybe it is just that."

I tipped my head to the side. "What are you talking about?"

"Maybe some of his struggle in trying to wrap his head around whatever you told him has to do with him not knowing how you feel."

"I've told him how I feel." Well, not really. I grimaced. "Okay, not exactly, but close enough."

"I've known him all my life. Mitch rarely has trouble working things out in any situation if he's solid on his feet. Have you considered him not knowing you love him is putting him on rocky ground? I know that's his weak spot."

"Explain." Weak spot?

"If he's sure of his position, he can make decisions. If he doesn't know you love him, it could be affecting how he thinks he should react to whatever it is you told him."

I hadn't considered that possibility. "You think it'd help if I told him how I feel?"

"I think it would go a long way in helping him work things out."

"Helping him? How much more am I supposed to do to help him? What about me? I've opened myself quite a bit here. How much more am I expected to do?"

"Isn't he worth it?" She asked before spinning around and striding toward the back door. She called over her shoulder, "I think he is."

I stood there for several moments considering what she'd said. Was Mitch struggling to accept me and my past because he wasn't sure how strongly I felt for him? Would telling him how much I loved him make that much of a difference? Was I strong enough? *Drat it.* I tipped my head back and inhaled a long deep breath. Closing my lids, I lifted my head and exhaled slowly. I am strong enough. One more chance to take. One more risk. But it'll be the last one. If it didn't help change things, that would be that. I'd get through the heartbreak, somehow. But, if I don't try, then I'll never know. I headed upstairs to shower and feed Harmony. Normally, Mitch closed for the night around nine. I checked the clock. I had time to get ready, meditate, then make my way to his house and still leave him around thirty minutes to unwind from work before facing me. A face off. Yeah, sure.

Around nine-thirty that night, I stood outside Mitch's house. Smoothing my shirt down, I let my hand press against my stomach. Now or never, I suppose. I knocked and waited, holding my breath. Faint sounds of steps approached the door from inside. He opened the door and his mouth dropped open. Guess he's surprised to see me. Was it a good idea to catch him off guard? I clenched my jaw. Too late now. I pasted a smile across my face.

"May I come in?"

He nodded, stepped back and closed the door behind me after I entered. He turned, heading into his kitchen and I followed. "Would you like something to drink?" He asked over his shoulder.

"Some wine would be nice," I answered. A little liquid courage never hurt. I sat at the marble countertop as he opened a bottle of wine, grabbed two glasses and poured. I sipped the woody floral blend, ordering my pounding heart to ease up trying to burst from my chest. Dark rings under his eyes contrasted sharply with the paleness of his cheeks.

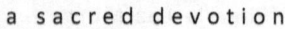

His normally tanned skin appeared tight where it peeked around his growing beard and mustache. Although my body yearned for his warmth, I held it in check and swallowed a large gulp of wine. Mitch's brows rose at the size of my gulp. I jerked a shoulder and stiffened my back. Deliberately setting down the glass, I placed both palms on the counter and leaned forward, staring directly into his eyes.

"I love you."

He jerked back and blinked.

Ha. Didn't expect that, did you? I continued. "I love you so much, I believed it was necessary to tell you everything about me and my past so you would know what I've been through. I wanted you to understand me. I opened myself to you to show you how much I trust you and love you. It wasn't easy to do that. In fact, it was hard as hell laying my heart and safety on the line like that. But you are worth it to me. You're worth risking everything."

"I—"

"No, wait, please," I interrupted. "Let me finish before I run out of courage to do so. If you can return my love, or can't or won't, I'll try to understand. But if you do love me as much as I love you, then I need to know you will stand beside me with my ability...gift...whatever you want to call it. If you can't or won't, then perhaps it's best we don't see each other anymore. We'll call these last ten months a nice time, but it would only be that and let it go. I won't hold a grudge. I'll only ask that you keep my secret out of respect of me."

He scooted around the counter and stood very close to me. His mossy scented body filled my head with memories of our lovemaking. He wrapped his arms around my shoulders, dropping his forehead to rest against mine.

"This whole time I've been thinking of how I could live without you. I can't. I love you too much to lose you. I'll keep your secret for you and hope you know I'd never do anything to hurt you or disappoint you. I promise I've got your back, no matter what."

The tears broke through and I let them. His mouth so close to mine made me want to kiss him and hold him tighter. I wrapped my arms around him and squeezed tightly.

"Oh, Mitch. I've missed you so much."

"Not as much as I've missed you, baby. I'm so sorry for going away and staying away from you."

I leaned back allowing only about an inch between our faces. "Don't ever do that again," I demanded.

"Never again," he said.

My gaze dropped to his mouth. It'd been so long since we'd been together it seemed like years instead

of weeks. "I need to kiss him." I gasped. *I'd said that out loud.*

"Go ahead, I won't tell," he whispered.

So, I did.

Chapter Nineteen

My mind blanked when my body got bombarded with sensations of sweet heat zinging through my veins, shoving away all the coldness from the very depths of my soul. I'd missed this so very much. Mitch's kiss acted like ambrosia and balm to the wounds left raw from the events of this last week. I kissed him back with everything I had in me, running my fingers through his hair, gripping and holding on when my legs weakened and threatened to collapse. His strong arms wrapped around my waist, lifting me and I wrapped my legs around his waist. He walked, holding me close to him and still held on when we dropped onto his bed. Yes. This. His touch and whispers both eased my muscles while at the same time kicking my pulse into high gear. The man had awesome moves. There in the darkness, we touched, kissed and showed each other how deep our love existed.

Later, the moonlight peeked through his bedroom curtains landing on the bare skin of his chest. The tips of my fingers trailed each spot in small circles while

my grin made my cheeks ache. I couldn't stop. I didn't want to.

"I wish we could stay here forever," I whispered.

"Marry me," he said.

I paused in my finger drawing to search his face. "Seriously?"

"I wouldn't ask if I didn't mean it, babe."

"Yes, but on one condition."

"Uh oh," he turned to his side and lifted my chin for a quick kiss. "What?"

"We have a long engagement, please."

"Why?"

"I think we need to live together for a bit, first."

"I expected you to move in, anyway. But how long of an engagement?"

"Can we give it at least a year?"

He squinted, and then shrugged. "Yes, if you live with me."

"Everyone will know I'm living here. You can accept that?" I leaned up. "Wait, you're not proposing so that our living together will be some kind of proper thing, are you?"

He sat. "Absolutely not. I want to marry you, but I'm willing to wait if you're living here with me. It has nothing to do with what the rest of the town might think."

"There's going to be gossip either way."

"Yes, but I'm only thinking of myself, to be honest. The rest of this town can simply accept it."

"Okay, then."

"When?" He asked.

"When what?"

"When will you move in? Tomorrow? I can have Zach cover my shift and I'll help you bring everything over here."

I laughed and flopped on my back watching the moonbeams cutting through the darkness of the room.

"Um, I might not be the only one moving in."

"What do you mean?" he asked lying down and curling next to me.

"I mean, I have Harmony. I think she'd prefer to stay at the shop. But in case she wants to come along, would you mind?"

"I'm okay with that, as long as she can be kept out of the kitchen."

"I'm thinking she'll probably want to stay at Trinkets." I rolled over and tapped his chest. "You know what that means, right?"

"What?"

"Maggie can take the apartment above the shop. It's a perfect solution for her."

"Great idea."

I hopped out of bed grabbing for my phone, when Mitch tugged me back. My phone slipped to the floor. "I wanted to call her and tell her the good news," I said.

"Nope. It's late. We both need sleep if we're moving everything tomorrow. You can tell her then," he said dropping kisses along my shoulder.

I trembled, as all thoughts of Maggie floated away. "Mm, yes," I whispered and turned toward him again.

****

The next morning, I dressed after having a very delightful, heated extra-long shower with Mitch. He kissed me as he strode out of the room and called over his shoulder.

"I'll make breakfast after I call Zach and ask him to cover my shift."

I happened to glance at the large bathroom mirror, noting all the red marks along my skin from Mitch's ardent and thorough attention last night. Thank goodness he shaved this morning. A grinning fool stared back at me and I shrugged. Finishing getting ready, I skipped to the kitchen as Mitch broke several eggs in a bowl. "What're we having?"

"I think we'll have some Belgian waffles. By then, the shop should be open, and we can give Maggie the good news together, if that's good with you?"

"Sounds like a great idea," I said beaming.

Epilogue

Hand in hand, Mitch and I left our house. Our house. Yes. Gotta remember that. So odd, but in a good way. As we walked down the street toward Main, I waited for him to drop my hand. He didn't. He kept it in his as we strolled across the street and turned heading toward Trinkets. I slid a quick glance toward the diner and more than one set of eyes watched us. Let them see me and my fiancé. Yep. That's us. I bit the inside of my cheek to keep the goofy grin threatening to spread across my face from doing so. Once we reached the shop, he opened the door for me, and we walked in. Maggie stood at the sales counter flipping through a stack of papers. I checked inside and no customers yet. Good. As we approached, she stopped and stared at us before breaking into a bright smile.

"Good morning, you two."

"Good morning," I said brightly, barely able to contain my grin. "Mitch and I have something to tell you.

Maggie tipped her head and her gaze swiftly looked down at my hand before returning to my face. "And that is?"

"We're engaged," Mitch said, then I held up a hand when she squealed. "Wait. We want to keep it quiet for now."

Maggie frowned. "Why?"

"Personal reasons," Mitch said.

"We're only telling you right now as it will affect you."

"How so?" She asked.

I wrapped an arm around her shoulder, "Because I'll be moving out to live with Mitch, so the apartment upstairs will be empty."

Maggie gasped. "No way."

I nodded. "Yes, way. Your apartment hunting is at an end. You can live up there, which will be close to town, like you wanted."

"Oh my gosh," she cried. "I can't believe it."

"You deserve it," I said.

She grabbed me in a big hug and held on tightly, whispering in my ear. "Thank you so very much."

Mitch coughed then said, "Pretty sweet deal, since you're only nineteen."

Maggie stepped out of our embrace and planted her hands on her hips. "I turned nineteen eight months ago, so I'll be twenty soon."

I gasped. "I missed your birthday?"

"We were still getting to know each other. It's okay."

"But twenty. Wow."

"Yep and since I start my second year in school this fall, the location is perfect. I can work the shop and attend online classes all in one building."

"All around a great idea," I said nudging Mitch. He glanced at me and strode towards the back.

"Where's he going?" Maggie asked.

"To let Andy know. You two will be the only ones right now. We'll make an announcement later when I'll have time to plan the wedding."

She hugged me again. "I'm so glad things worked out between you two."

"Me too," I said. "You going to be okay here alone?"

She nodded. "Yeah. Busy tourist time won't be for another month or so, which will leave me plenty of time to get organized, settled and be able to visit my grandma, make sure she's settling in okay."

"Perfect." I shifted, scanning the back area where Mitch reappeared holding several boxes. "I guess I'll go grab my personal things today."

Together we joined Mitch. "I'll help too since we're slow," Maggie offered.

"Thanks. I'll hit my office, if you'll do my closet? I'll leave the food in the kitchen for you."

"Thanks, that'll help. Is it okay if I redecorate?"

"Do whatever you'd like. I'm not taking the furniture, except for the couch from my office. I hope you can use them. If not, we can always store them in the basement," I said as we hiked the stairs.

"I'll use them, trust me. I'm not a big furniture shopper for myself. I'll use what you leave."

"I'll get your dresser. You have a suitcase, right?" Mitch asked.

"Yes, in the closet."

At the top of the stairs, we each went our separate ways to pack. As I entered the office, I set the box on the couch and headed toward the window to peer out at the scene below. Almost a year now here in this town. Somehow, I knew I'd miss this view. Mitch entered behind me.

"All done, and I loved doing the intimate drawer."

I grinned. "I bet you did."

"I called Bobby and he's going to lend us his truck for a larger load. You don't want any of the furniture here?"

I shook my head. "Only this couch," I pointed to the purple colored piece I'd laid in many times contemplating my life here. "I want that in my office at the house."

148

"You got it. You need help in here?"

"If you'd like to start with the bookshelves, I'd appreciate it. I'll do my desk."

For the next few hours, we packed, cleaned and organized the rest of my things in the spare room. Harmony made her tour around and settled on the couch. I stroked her softly. "I'll see you soon," I said and grabbed a box heading out. Mitch and I each carried a box and strolled home. Good thing my box was light. Poor Mitch grabbed the heavier box. "You doing okay? I know that's heavy."

"I'm fine and it's not that heavy," he said.

"If you say so." After arriving home, he placed the boxes from my old office into my new one.

"I'm going to go back and grab your suitcase, so there's no pressure in getting the rest of your items until we get Bobby's truck."

"Sounds like a fine idea," I responded watching him leave.

I tugged the box he'd carried and opened it near my new desk. Sliding the flaps open, I slipped on my gloves and lifted my box of trinkets. Setting it in the bottom right drawer, I tugged off my gloves and laid them across the cover. Leaning back in my chair, I gazed out the picture window across from me. This will work. *It will.* I just need to figure out how to keep Mitch from finding out about Steph's ghostly

existence. Nope. I shook my head. Not going there right now. Right now, I'm where I want to be for a very long time. I'm finally home.

ABOUT THE AUTHOR

Sherrie Lea Morgan is an active member of Romance Writers of America and her local Chapter Georgia Romance Writers. She lives north of Atlanta, GA with her twin sister, two dogs and two cats. Her goal is to encourage readers to see ghosts in a different way. When not working her current manuscripts, she enjoys spending time with her sister, daughter and son. Although her children refuse to join her paranormal movie thrills, they are supportive in her obsession of all things scary. Of course, they are always willing to travel with her.

www.sherrieleamorgan.com

https://www.facebook.com/sherrielea.morgan

https://mobile.twitter.com/slmorganwrit

www.ingramcontent.com/pod-product-compliance
Lightning Source LLC
Chambersburg PA
CBHW021100130626
46552CB00005B/2190